Missed Her

Missed Her

stories by

Ivan E. Coyote

ARSENAL PULP PRESS | VANCOUVER

ARSENAL PULP PRESS
Suite 101, 211 East Georgia St.
Vancouver, BC
Canada V6A 1Z6
arsenalpulp.com

The publisher gratefully acknowledges the support of the Canada
Council for the Arts and the British Columbia Arts Council for
its publishing program, and the Government of Canada (through
the Canada Book Fund) and the Government of British Columbia
(through the Book Publishing Tax Credit Program) for its publishing
activities.

This is a work of fiction. Any resemblance of characters to persons
either living or deceased is purely coincidental.

Earlier versions of these stories appeared in *Xtra! West*

Cover photograph by Dan Bushnell
Photograph of Ivan E. Coyote by Eric Nielson
Letter on the back cover by Patricia Cumming Sr.
Book design by Shyla Seller

Printed and bound in Canada on 100% PCW recycled paper

Library and Archives Canada Cataloguing in Publication:

Coyote, Ivan E. (Ivan Elizabeth), 1969-
         Missed her / Ivan E. Coyote.

Issued also in an electronic format.
ISBN 978-1-55152-371-2

     I. Title.

PS8555.O99M57 2010   C813'.6   C2010-904286-7

Mixed Sources
Product group from well-managed forests,
controlled sources and recycled wood or fiber
www.fsc.org Cert no. SW-COC-000952
© 1996 Forest Stewardship Council
FSC

This book is dedicated to Florence Amelia Mary Daws
October 21st, 1919 – May 13th, 2009
thank you Gran, for keeping us all together.

Acknowledgments

I would like to thank my family, again, for allowing me to write my version of our stories down. I know I never get it quite right, but you can't say that I am not practicing. The more of the world I meet, the more I realize just how lucky I truly am to be from where I am from, and from whom I come from. Patricia Cumming, my grandmother, I will never forget the days we spent at your kitchen table unraveling bits of the story which appears in these pages, and the tea and the tears and the homemade soup we shared. Florence Daws, my grandmother, I feel truly blessed that I was able to be there with you and the rest of our family for your last days. Please know that I remember everything you taught me, and that pieces of you live on in the best parts of me. I miss you every single day.

I am most grateful to my mom, Patricia Daws, and my father, Don Cumming, for still loving me even though and in spite of and on top of it all. I promise to do the same.

I cannot write that this book would not exist if were not for my partner, Zena Sharman, because that would not be true. I will always write, no matter what is happening around me. I think this is what makes her love me, and I know that the kind of love we have built together makes me reach to be better. A better writer, a better partner, a better cook. Zena, you made the writing of this book easier, and more joyful. I promise I will keep the cupboards more organized while I am writing the next one. You are my family, too. Together, we are unstoppable.

I would like to acknowledge the ongoing work and support of Arsenal Pulp Press. Brian Lam, Robert Ballantyne, Shyla Seller,

Janice Beley and the staff of that little office have become like another family to me. For over a decade we have worked, laughed, conspired, planned, fought, and somehow created six books together. I am proud of Arsenal and the amazing work they do to bring relevant, revolutionary, marginalized and queer voices into the light and onto the shelves.

I must also thank each and every person who comes out to hear me tell stories on stage, who buys my books and reads my columns, who clicks play or share or forward on my behalf. You are making it possible for me to do this for a living, and I thank you.

I especially want to thank the kids in the schools I visit, for your brilliant questions and better-world-one-day eyes and the heart-bending letters you write me. I want to acknowledge the freaks and geeks and queers and kids who, for whatever reason, cannot wait for school to be over. I want to you know we will all be here waiting for you. You are evidence that we are, indeed, carving out some space for all of us.

What a big, wide, beautiful family I am blessed to be a part of.

Contents

Resident Expert 11

Nobody Ever 15

Cooling Down 19

Which Doctor 23

Je Suis Femme 27

Hair Today 31

This Summer, at Gay Camp 35

Let Me Show You 39

Good Old Days 43

Straighten Up 47

Boner Preservation Society 51

Objects in Mirror Are Queerer Than They Appear 56

Truth Story 60

Gifted 63

Talking to Strangers 68

The Rest of Us 73

A Butch Roadmap 77

Hats Off 81

Straight Teens Talk Queer 85

Some of My Best Friends are Rednecks 90

One Among the Many 94

Throwing in the Towel 98

On Angels and Afterlife 102

Uncle Ivan's Broken Hearts' Club Plan 106

The Butch Version 110

She Shoots, She Scores 114

Only Two Reasons 118

Maiden Heart 121

All about Herman 129

Just a Love Story 137

Resident Expert

This morning in the Ottawa Valley was crystal blue clear and cold, a nippley minus thirty-two degrees Celsius if you factor in the wind chill, which I have learned it is always best to do. I had just gotten home from the road, and was still a little jet-lagged, my body and mind hovering blearily somewhere on the clock between west coast and eastern standard time. I was definitely not prepared for what was about to happen.

I stopped by the old corner store for a coffee just after eight this morning, on the way into the city for my office hours. Most of the regulars were already there, bundled up and breathing bursts of white warm air in the frigid back room, drinking drip coffee with their gloves still on.

There was the usual round of hellos and catching up to do when I get home from a road trip, and then Dan, the salesman, cleared his throat and fixed his gaze on me.

"Hey Ivan, have you ever heard of a guy by the name of Buck Angel?"

I flipped through my mental rolodex, and felt my heart speed up a little. I had, indeed, heard of a guy by the name of Buck Angel. The problem was, I didn't really want to discuss Buck Angel in the backroom of the only store in my small town at eight o'clock in the morning. But I know Dan. Attempting to change the subject when questioned about a subject such as this one would only draw more attention to the subject I wish had never come up in the first place. Dan is a really nice guy, with a thirteen-year-old kid and a wife battling ovarian cancer. He likes classic rock and his surround sound stereo system and comic books and golf. He is not supposed to know who Buck Angel is, and I am not supposed to have to be the one to explain it all to him.

"Uh, yeah, I think I have," I said, my voice cracking just a little. I silently cursed the Internet, and all that it makes available to everyone, no matter how far out of town they are living. "Are you referring to Buck Angel, the transsexual internet porn star?" My face and ears felt like they were about to spontaneously combust.

Dan picked up the ball and rolled with it. Everybody but me leaned in close around the old wooden table, fascinated. "I saw him on that show *Sexcetera*. He's bald and tough, all full of muscles and covered with tattoos, a real scary-looking dude, I'd never pick a fight with him, anyways. And then..." he waggled all ten of his digits in the air in front of his face for emphasis, then raised his eyebrows and aimed both index fingers in the direction of his crotch. "Bingo bango, there it is. Dude has a vagina. The Man With A Pussy, he calls himself. Totally freaked me out."

There was a round of exclamation points and guffaws of disbelief. Men with pussies was big news out here in the country. Only two of us at the table were noticeably silent on this matter, namely Patrick, one half of the only gay couple in town, and myself, who was seriously considering bolting for the back door. The only thing keeping my ass in my chair was the fact that running from the topic at hand would probably look bad.

I swallowed what little spit I had left in my mouth and said nothing. Clayton, the beef farmer, broke the moment of silence for me.

"So tell us, Dan, was he hot or not?"

Another round of hysterics broke out. Gwen, the office administrator, had sat down halfway through the story, and she looked a little confused. She narrowed her eyes at Dan.

"What the hell have you been Googling this time?" She, too, blamed the Internet.

Dan shook his head; his palms held up, empty, pleading innocence. "I saw it on the television, I swear to God. There was also a bit on the same show about the technique of fellatio. Fascinating stuff."

"Oh, so it's like an educational program?" quipped Pete, the guy who takes care of the skating rink. "Well, good for you, Dan, always seeking out knowledge. I'm proud of you."

"Fellatio instructions, heh? On television?" Brian, the fireman, raised his eyebrow. "So, Dan, are you getting any better?"

Dan blushed. We all laughed.

"And here I had to go out and learn the hard way." This, of course, came from Patrick, and almost caused poor Pete to spray coffee out his nostrils.

And just like that, the topic shifted, and we moved on. As I drove into town later, I pondered the whole ordeal, and second-guessed my panicked reaction. Maybe I should have seized upon this excellent learning opportunity, and taken it upon myself to educate my neighbours about trans issues. But it was eight o'clock in the morning, I argued with myself on behalf of myself, I hadn't even had a full cup of coffee yet. Besides, here I was, living my life with my head held up and making no apologies in a town without a gas station, much less a gay bar. Wasn't I already doing my bit? It only made sense that I would naturally be the one to come to with questions when it came to topics such as burly men sporting tattoos and vaginas, but I couldn't be expected to have rehearsed and memorized all the perfect things to say all the time, could I? I consoled myself with the knowledge that whenever I failed to come up with the right answers for my new neighbours' questions, they could always turn to the Internet, or at the very least, their cable TV.

Nobody Ever

It was raining the day I met her. The kind of rain that hits the pavement and puddles so hard it bounces back at the sky, backward and defiant. It was the kind of evening best spent inside, but there she was, standing soggy on the sidewalk, waiting to talk to me.

As soon as I emerged from the back door of the theatre, she speed-walked in a straight line towards me. Her name was Ruby, she told me, and she was from a small town, about three hours' drive from here. She was almost twelve years old and she wanted to be a firefighter when she grew up, or maybe a marine biologist. Her mom had driven her here, so she could see me perform at the Capitol Theater. It had said on my website that I was going to be reading in Olympia, Washington, and since it was a Saturday and there was no school she had made her mom drive her all this way for my show, but then it turned out that since they were selling alcohol in the theatre she wasn't allowed inside, not until she turned twenty-one, anyways, which was like, ten years away, practically.

She took a deep breath, and continued. She had seen

me at the folk festival in Vancouver last summer, and I had read a story about a tomboy I had met at the farmers' market, did I remember the one?

I nodded, yes, I did.

She shifted her weight from one sneakered foot to the other and back again, like she needed to pee, and flipped her head back to shake her shaggy bangs out of her eyes. She blurted out her words like machine gun bullets, like she had been rehearsing them for a while, her mouth pursed in a determined little raisin.

When she first heard that story, well, she was just amazed, she told me. She had begged her mom to buy her all of my books right there on the spot, but her mom only had enough money for one. She had to wait until it was her birthday, which was October by the way, until she could get my next book, and then she got one more from her aunt at Christmas, but when was I going to put out a new one? She liked them all, nearly the same amount, except for *Loose End,* which of course was her favourite because it had the story "Saturdays and Cowboy Hats" in it, which was the very first story of mine she ever found out about, when she heard me at the park in Vancouver last summer but she had already told me that part.

By this time I was ready to scoop Ruby up in my arms and hug her, but I didn't, because her mom was waiting in the car parked two feet away from where we were standing and I thought it might seem weird.

Ruby stepped sideways, farther under the awning over the door of the theatre. She pulled a love-worn copy of my book out from her rain jacket, and held it out to me.

"Could you sign it for me? To Ruby, Love from Ivan? You could say, To my biggest fan, Ruby, too, if you felt like it. Whatever you want."

I wrote "to Ruby, my biggest fan, Love from your biggest fan, Ivan," and passed it back to her. She tucked it under her armpit for safekeeping. Her fingernails were bitten right down to the quick, just like mine used to be.

"Thanks. I really love your books a lot. Especially the one about the tomboy, cuz, well, the little girl in that story, she reminds me of me." She paused for a second, met my eyes with hers, and held them there. "And nobody ever reminds me of me."

I stepped back out into the rain, hoping that it would look like raindrops sliding down my cheeks, not big hot tears. I pulled one of my CDs out of my bag and passed it to her.

"Here you go, this should hold you until the new book is out."

The last time I saw Ruby, she was waving backwards at me from the passenger seat of a beat-up station wagon. Her mom honked the horn twice goodbye as they turned and disappeared around the corner.

A while ago I was reading at a fundraising dinner in Ottawa, and I met a woman named Hilary. Hilary was in her fifties I would say, wearing black boots and old jeans. She used to own her own house painting company, but she was retired now. I liked how she shook my hand too hard, how the skin of her palms was still callused, how she spooned too much sugar into her coffee. I liked how she ate her salad with her dinner fork and didn't care. Her hair was just getting long enough to brush the collar of her dress shirt and hang over the tops of her ears. This probably bothered her, and she probably had an appointment to get it cut early next week, before it got totally out of hand.

After the gig was over, she helped me pack the rest of my books out to my truck. We talked about everything and nothing: what it used to be like working on a job site twenty years ago, how it is better now but not by much, what a difference a good pair of snow tires can make, how the old back just ain't what it used to be, stuff like that.

The snow was falling in fat lazy flakes. The parking lot was empty, except for two trucks, one hers, the other mine. Finally, she shook my hand hard one last time and then pulled me into a hug.

"Make sure you keep in touch," she told me. "It was great to meet you. You remind me of me when I was a kid."

Cooling Down

I call her my niece, even though technically she isn't. She is my cousin Dan's wife's daughter from another relationship, but in my family that makes her my niece. I'm too old for her to call me her cousin, and too butch to be her aunt, so that makes me Uncle Ivan. Just like my cousin Trish in Toronto is really my Dad's mom's brother's daughter, which I think would make her my second cousin, but to me she is just cousin Trish. Sometimes, with my family, it's not so much about blood in the veins as it is water under the bridge.

The first time I met my new niece-to-be she was five or so, wearing a striped T-shirt and shorts. It was the heyday of those razor scooter things, and she was scooting industriously up and down the cracked sidewalk outside of my cousin's apartment. Dan and I were standing in the long and sideways summer shadows of the trees in the park across the street, talking.

She rolled up beside me, braking skillfully. Dan introduced us, and then my future niece said the most awesome first line I think I've ever heard from a kid:

"You wanna see my calluses?"

Of course I wanted to see her calluses. She went on to explain that she had been practicing a lot on the monkey bars, and had in fact just today broken her all-time monkey bar record of over two hours without ever letting her feet touch the ground.

I was duly impressed with her accomplishments, and told her so. She made a little small talk and then excused herself. "Well, gotta get back at it," she announced with a deep exhale. Apparently scooter skills such as hers required dedication and sacrifice as well.

She scootered off, the tip of her pink tongue placed determinedly between her lips.

"Why didn't you tell me?" I asked him. "You said Sarah had a kid, you didn't mention she was the fucking coolest kid ever."

"I know. She's something else, huh?" Dan smiled proudly. I knew he had taken to soaking his smelly feet in scented water before his dates with Sarah, and had even started wearing underwear and changing the sheets. There was something special about this new girl and her über-cool daughter. They were going to be around for a while.

Somehow, inexplicably, that was almost ten years ago. Dan and Sarah are married, and Layla is now fifteen, and just got her cell phone confiscated for not telling the truth and smoking cigarettes.

I went out for dim sum with her and Dan when I was in town last week. I had just spent the better part of the last three months sweating through a cold turkey nicotine withdrawal. I swirled shrimp dumplings in spicy yellow mustard, and described the first two weeks of insomnia, followed by a month of anxiety and random attacks of un-explained nervousness, topped off by a good six weeks of alternating crying jags and unfocused housecleaning.

"I'm not going to lie to you and say I don't miss smok-ing," I tell her. "And I'm not going to give you some bullshit line about how smoking isn't cool."

"Smoking is cool," Dan agrees. "I loved it."

I nod in agreement.

"But if I had it to do all over again, I never ever would have started," I tell her. "Think yellow teeth. Think smelly clothes. Think about how much longer it will take you to save up for that digital camera you want. Think of the non-smokers who won't want to kiss you. Then when you're done thinking about all that, it will be time to consider the can-cer."

I remember this time when I was about fifteen, sleep-ing the afternoon away, when I was awakened by my cool Uncle John.

"I love you," he whispered. "And that's why I woke you up to tell you to quit smoking that stuff. Take it from me." His breath smelled like beer and his flannel shirt smelled like cigarettes. "Do yourself a favour."

I didn't listen to him then, just like Layla wasn't listen-ing to me now.

I was supposed to be the cool uncle. I was supposed to be the one she could come and talk to about stuff she couldn't go to any of her four parents about. I was supposed to hook her up with wine coolers and let her smoke pot in my rec room and get her concert tickets for Christmas. I had the tattoos and everything. Instead I was giving her a lecture about smoking, something I had seen fit to do myself for most of my adult life, until a mere four months ago. Just when had I become so totally uncool?

And wait, it gets worse. Layla made the mistake of telling me that her great grandpa had left her a small inheritance, and that she planned to spend it traveling around Europe for a couple of years after she finished high school.

"I want to, you know, see the world and stuff, before I go to college. Just in case I get into an accident or something, and can't get around."

I shook my head violently. I couldn't believe the words my mouth was making, even as they passed over my lips. "You really should think about taking that money and investing it in yourself. You should spend it on school, so that you get an education, which will get you a good job, so you can travel later in life whenever you want."

I believe my mother had given me this exact speech, some twenty odd years ago.

Just then my girlfriend called me on my cell phone. She's almost done her PhD. I passed the phone to Layla, hoping she could convince my niece of the value of an education.

"Nothing much," Layla says. "Dan and Ivan are just telling me how I should open up a savings account before I go to Europe."

That is not at all what I was just saying. In one ear and out the other. Kids these days.

Which Doctor

I spent the better part of the last six weeks on the road, and it finally caught up to me. Over twenty gigs and twelve airplane rides in forty days, and finally my carbon footprint kicked me in the ass. I woke up the first morning home with a throat full of razor blades and a fever, and two days later a nasty green monster had taken up residence in my chest.

A week later it was worse, not better. My girlfriend, my mother, and the little old lady across the street were all in agreement—I needed to go see the doctor and get me some pills. At least get myself checked out, since there were some nasty things going around, and it was best not to take any chances.

I have had the same doctor in Vancouver for the last eighteen years. She never blinks an eye at my tattoos, or my chest hair. She is unfazed by piercings. As much as I hate going to the doctor, I have learned to love and respect her over the years. She works at a clinic on Commercial Drive. She calls me Ivan. She knows I'm queer and couldn't care less. She reads my books. The only thing she has ever questioned me about is smoking cigarettes, and even then all she did was ask me if there was anything she could do to help me quit.

But I wasn't sick in Vancouver, I was sick in a small Ontario hamlet that doesn't even have its own gas station, much less a queer- and trans-positive walk-in clinic. Every time I tried to imagine driving myself twenty minutes into Arnprior and taking off my shirt in front of a strange doctor in a small town, a prickly lump of panic would swell up in my chest. I could see it unfolding like a homo horror movie plot in my mind: the doctor walking into the waiting room with my chart in his hand, and calling out my legal name, and then doing a double take when I stood up to follow him. Even though all I needed was a stethoscope on my chest, in my nightmare I am naked except for a paper dress, on my back on the examination bed with my icy feet in the stirrups, trying to explain my complicated gender identity to an aging ex-military doctor with a brush cut and still muscular forearms. There are needlepoint Bible verses framed and hung on the walls of his office. His wife likes to do needlepoint, when she isn't teaching Sunday school or volunteering on the right-to-life pregnancy hotline. I am crying and he is frowning.

It probably wouldn't have been anywhere near this terrifying, but I am cursed with an active imagination. So I didn't go.

Ten days later, I still wasn't getting better. My girlfriend sent me a link to a walk-in clinic in downtown Ottawa. There were rainbow flags all over the home page of their website, so I called to see if I could book myself an appointment. The receptionist explained to me that I lived outside of their catchment area, and would have to find somewhere closer to where I lived. I told her I was living in a very small town, and that I didn't really fit into a gender box, and that I was a bit afraid to go to a small-town doctor. She told me I was just going to have to get over my social phobia if I wanted medical attention.

I swallowed, not quite believing what I had just heard. I thanked her for all her help, letting the sarcasm seep into my voice, and hung up the phone. I paced back and forth across the kitchen floor twenty times or so, trying not to let the tears spill over my bottom lids, then picked up the phone and hit redial. I asked to speak to the clinic's director, and explained to her what had just happened.

To her credit, she was as horrified as I was by what I had just been told. She apologized profusely and assured me that a terrible mistake had been made, and that she would talk to the receptionist and make sure that nothing like this ever happened again. She said that because I worked in Ottawa, I could come in the next day and see a doctor. A doctor who didn't care if I had chest hair and a girlfriend.

All the way into the city the next morning, I thought about it all. I've heard the stories. Trans men who are saving up for top surgery and haven't had a breast examination or a mammogram in years because they felt the same prickly lump of panic in their chest at the thought of a stranger touching the breasts they didn't like to be reminded that they still had. The lump of panic weighed more than the lump the doctor would be feeling around for, so they didn't go. Trans women with prostate glands afraid of judgmental doctors with unkind hands. All those bodies that belong to my people, people who have learned ways to hide their breasts and tuck their penis away and shave and pluck and bind parts of themselves. People who can't be touched in certain places by their lovers in the dark, much less a stranger in a white coat under a fluorescent glow. When was the last time I had a pap test?

I thought of all the small-town queers and trans folks out there, who don't have access to the (sometimes) progressive-minded inner city clinics that fly the rainbow flag, because their postal code gets in the way. I realized that finding a doctor who I felt comfortable and safe with was only the first step. The hardest part was convincing myself to go.

Je Suis Femme

I used to have two dogs: Deja, a big hairy old husky mix, and the little guy named Goliath, a Pekinese-Pomeranian cross with a foreskin abnormality. I gave him a tough name not only because he would go on to weigh eight pounds when full-grown, but also because his penis can't descend like the penises of other, less special dogs do. When he gets an erection, which is often, instead of a little lipstick appearing, he gets a lump in his tummy.

Three months ago Deja, my old lady dog, passed away after fifteen years of friendship and shedding. So now it's just me and the little guy. Goliath and I had a hard time adjusting at first, him wandering around the house looking for his friend and me trying not to cry every time I swept the hairless floor, but slowly we are getting used to life without the old dog. I have taken a bit of flak in the past for being a butch with a fluffy little dog on a leash, but then the big dog would run up with a giant stick in her mouth and whoever was hassling me would back down, their masculine image of me somehow repaired and intact again. Having one big dog and one little one was kind of like those guys who drive a mini-van with two car seats in the back and a bumper sticker that says, "My other car is a Harley." Deja was my Harley, but she's gone now. The other day a butch friend of mine met Goliath for the first time, and she laughed out loud, right in his fluffy face, which was right beside my face, because I was holding him under my arm.

"I never pictured you with a lap dog," she smirked.

"I am a multi-faceted and complex individual," I told her.

She snorted.

"My truck is bigger than yours," I retorted, which shut her up.

Later that night, in a bar in Ottawa, she offered to buy me a beer.

"I can't drink beer, I am gluten intolerant," I explained, hating the way this sounded before it even left my mouth.

She raised an eyebrow. "How about a white wine then?"

"How about I kick your ass?"

She bought me a vodka and cranberry juice, which came with a thin pink straw and smiled smugly at me for the rest of the night from behind a butch-looking pint of dark beer.

My girlfriend was in town last weekend, and we ran into an old co-worker of hers on the street, a professional lesbian in a smart two-piece pantsuit. Small talk was exchanged, and then we parted ways.

"Have you ever met her partner?" I asked my sweetheart.

"Once, at a wine-and-cheese type thing. She and her girlfriend were both wearing skirts. It kind of freaked me out."

I shuddered. "What do you think they do in bed?"

My girlfriend shrugged, and then we laughed. We both know already that we are a little old school when it comes to things like all-femme action or butch-on-butch love. It's not that I don't completely support the rights of others to do what they want with whomever is consenting; it's just that it's not how I am wired. The landscape my libido responds to is curvy and wears lipstick, and is attracted to biceps and big black boots.

I took my curvy and lipsticked lady friend to Montreal last weekend for a romantic getaway. We walked and shopped and fucked and ate and walked some more. My new big black boots were killing my feet, but I tried to keep this to myself. My sweetheart went to French immersion school when she was a kid, whereas I was a lucky participant in a pilot project where I learned Tlingit, a First Nations language spoken mostly in the Southern Yukon. Learning Tlingit was cool, but not so handy later in life when ordering cappuccinos in Montreal. I did study some French in high school and I have had a few Québécois girlfriends over the years, so I mostly understand the gist of a conversation, but I often freeze up a little when it comes to actually speaking it, especially when nervous or overly sober. I'm more of a listener *en français*, which I like to think of as a welcome change of pace from my English self.

On our last morning in Montreal I managed to mumble my way through ordering two medium coffees, one orange juice, and a bottle of water in French, and then ducked into the women's washroom. There were two middle-aged ladies washing their hands, which they immediately began to wave in my face as they cursed me in what I can only guess was most likely French, pushing me with their words backwards toward the bathroom door as they advanced.

I panicked, forgetting even how to speak much English for a minute. I fumbled frantically around in my head for the right words in French. The only words I could find were simple, a baby sentence, lacking in grammar or style, which I blurted out crudely, my last defence:

"Je suis femme." What I meant to say was I'm sorry, and I don't mean to frighten or alarm you, but contrary to what you seem to think, I am a predominately estrogen-based organism and I wish to avail myself of the facilities. What I actually said was, "I am woman."

They both stopped for a millisecond, looked at each other and then back at me, and continued to scold me out the door. I turned and bolted for the men's room, which seemed to have been hosed down with stale urine and was out of toilet paper. Someone had also borrowed the stall door and toilet seat and forgot to return them. Next time I need to use the *salle de bain*, I will have to remember to bring a pink cocktail and my little dog.

Hair Today

I had the same barber in Vancouver for fifteen years. When he left Commercial Drive for the West End, I mourned him like a long-time lover. A less than satisfying roll in the hay with a stranger I can shake off in a couple of days, but a bad haircut, well, that shit takes time to heal.

When I first got to Ottawa, I made the mistake of stumbling into a fancy salon in gaytown. My bangs were hanging over my eyes, I couldn't see my own ears, and I was desperate. Eighty dollars plus tip and a disturbingly sensual mint-and-rosemary-infused scalp massage later, I emerged back onto Bank Street with a slightly more effeminate replica of the hairdo I had walked in with, approximately three-and-one-half millimeters shorter than it was when I woke up that morning. It looked great for about four days, then I needed a haircut again. It was a great consumer experience, but at that rate it was going to cost me approximately six hundred bucks a month to keep my bangs out of my eyes. I needed a barber. A good, old-fashioned, wait-your-turn-twelve-bucks-take-a-little-off-the-top kind of guy like the one I used to have back home.

I found him at the other end of Bank Street. A sun-faded swirling barber's pole led to a staircase, which turned into a narrow hallway humbly covered in decades-old carpet hammered down by thousands of work boots and dress shoes, a worn-out roadmap that directed me to a doorway.

You know you've got the right place by the smell. Old Spice-scented men's talc, cologne, that weird blue stuff they dip the combs in, and the leftover waft of someone smoking a cigar late last night when everyone had gone home and the doors were all locked up for the day.

My new barber is Lebanese, with hands the size of small hams, boasting a handshake that could crack a walnut. The first time I went in, I brought my sweetheart with me. This turned out to be an accidentally brilliant move. She is, of course, gorgeous, and her silver curls and dimples bought me the kind of street cred that a barely bicepped, moustacheless guy like me needs when being introduced to all the good old boys from the neighbourhood. Maybe I am a soft-spoken young fellow with long eyelashes, or maybe I am one of those kinds of women who could never land herself a good man. Who knows what they are thinking. But at least my girlfriend is hot.

"Sit down right here, boss." He always calls everyone boss. "And will you take a look at your lady friend? What a beautiful girl."

He got no argument from me. I'm not sure exactly what it feels like for her to be talked about in the third person when she is actually present to overhear conversations about how attractive she is, but we both just assumed he meant well. Some would call this allowing my female partner to be treated as an object, and trading on patriarchal standards of female desirability in order to garner favour in a male-dominated environment. I call it getting a cheap haircut.

After he was finished giving me the perfect haircut in under ten minutes for a total of fifteen dollars with tip, he whipped off the towel around my neck with a flourish and held up a hand mirror for me to take a look at the back.

"Would you take a look at that? Handsome guy."

There is always a chance that at any point in this interaction something, and it could be anything, will tip the scales and whomever I am talking to will all of a sudden realize that I am not what they may have thought I was. They might not care at all. They might care a whole lot. They might change their body language, their tone of voice, or their mind about how much they like me. I have no control over any of this. My options are limited. I could choose to go about my everyday, ordinary, human business, and each and every time I interact with a perfect stranger I could say, "Hello, my name is Ivan and I need a haircut, car wash, library book, or a latte. In case you are wondering (are you wondering? Sometimes it is hard to tell. And in case maybe I am obligated, am I obligated? Who knows. Anyway...), I am a predominately estrogen-based organism. You may proceed to treat me thusly, based on how much you respect women, and how you feel inside about people who, even when forced into a gender box, refuse to close the lid.

But this would be unwieldy, none of their business, and most importantly, it would be a definite overshare. Mostly

I just try to be personable and polite, not assume anything about anyone, and hope for the best.

I went in for a haircut again before I left town. My barber went on at length about how much he missed my beautiful lady, and why was she breaking his heart by not coming in to visit more often?

"You are lucky guy, that such a beautiful girl loves you like that. I am going to tell you a secret, where to get a leg of lamb, the best butcher in all of Ottawa. You get a nice bottle of wine, okay, and make sure she keeps coming back here to see us?"

I asked him how long he had been married.

He shook his head, sweeping the back of my neck with a brush coated in talcum powder. "Me, boss? I been divorced now twenty-six years."

I laughed out loud, and asked him why I should take advice on keeping a quality woman around. Maybe I laughed like a girl. Although I highly doubt it. Maybe he finally noticed that I have wrinkles and grey hair, but still don't need to shave. Who can know what it was?

He stopped for a beat, his eyes meeting mine in my reflection in the mirror.

"You bring that lady in next time she comes to visit. You tell her I love her."

He held up the mirror in one hand and turned the chair so I could see the back of my neck.

"Look at that now." He smiled, patting my shoulder. "Aren't you beautiful too?"

This Summer, At Gay Camp

He shone like a brand new dime, that first time. "I want you to meet my son," she had told me. "I want him to meet more gay people. School has been hard on him these last couple of years."

I was in Fort Smith, Northwest Territories, on tour with a mismatched set of other storytellers. It was the first week of June, and the roof of the earth was gearing up for summer solstice. The midnight sun stretched the light so far and long that dusk was bent over backward enough to bump into the next day. The sun cooked the dirt into dust that got into everything, grinding between back teeth and turning my new black boots grey. We were a seven-hour drive by mostly gravel road to Yellowknife. A hell of a place to try to hide yourself. A hell of a place to have to repeat grade ten.

His mother was a solid, smiling Métis woman with a laugh you could hear from the other side of the lake. Her son stepped out of the car and onto the weary pavement of the parking lot outside of the only motel in town, which boasted a restaurant that served both Chinese and Italian cuisine, and I use the term loosely.

He was wearing brand new sneakers, so white they caught the sunlight and bounced it right back, bleaching the backs of my eyelids when I closed them. His tracksuit was also white, both pieces, and so was the singlet he had on underneath. All of his clothes were crisp and pristine, with a fresh-out-of-the-wrapper look that stood out stark and sudden against the frayed and aging backdrop of this little northern town.

He was sapling thin, with cover girl cheekbones and feather duster lashes. Easily one of the prettiest boys I had ever seen, all long fingers and fey hips and wrists. I could imagine him standing in a line-up on Davie Street in Vancouver, waiting to get into a club that would be pounding a dull bassline from inside, surrounded by his twinkie buddies in designer jeans and two-hundred-dollar T-shirts. That such a creature still breathed in a high school in Fort Smith, Northwest Territories, seemed somehow unfathomable to me.

A mud-coloured pick-up pulled up beside us, its tires popping bits of loose gravel sideways. Our hiking guide jumped down from the driver's seat, wearing sturdy boots and a grey beard. He led us on a meandering route past the old graveyard and down a well-worn path through the pines, wide shards of sunlight showing the dust and dandelion seeds floating in the air that smelled so much like home to me. I kept stealing looks at my friend's fairy boy son, him in his immaculate threads and me in my now dirty new Fleuvog boots and vintage leather coat. I loved him at first sight, flying his flaming flag so fiercely, here, so far from a pride parade or leather bar or Mac counter. All of fifteen years old and fearless already.

Later, I pulled his mother aside and told her about a camp in Edmonton for gay youth where I was going to be artist-in-residence in a couple of weeks. It was probably too late for this year, I told her, but what the hell, send in an application, because you never know.

The last week in July, he sashayed through the door of the education centre in Edmonton. Sixty-five queer youth for four days. I wondered if he had ever been around more than one or two queer people at the same time before. I wondered if he felt as overwhelmed as I did. A place where faggot wasn't a bad word anymore. A place where he could be one of many. A place where he could just be.

I got to work, teaching creative writing classes every morning and cajoling my group of youth to choreograph an a cappella synchronized dance number to "I Will Survive." He was in my group, and I spent the better part of four days trying not to hug him too much in front of everybody else.

On Saturday night there was a talent show. One of the local kids organized a fashion show, and he modeled a gold lamé gown complete with fake breasts and walked the runway in heels like he was born in them. I felt like the homosexual version of a hockey dad whose son has just scored in overtime.

I watched him stand taller and smile bigger and swish wider every day. And then, of course, the inevitable came around.

37

Sunday night. There was a lot of crying, the kind of tears that could only be conjured up by a bunch of queer kids about to return to High River and Moose Jaw and some little town just north of Edmonton. Alone.

I couldn't even look him in the eyes the last time I hugged him. I couldn't tell him what I was thinking. I hoped that the new pride he held in his shoulders wasn't going to be pounded out of him in gym class, or while he tried to learn trigonometry. I felt sad, but mostly I felt rage.

Rage that we are beginning the second decade of the twenty-first century in what is supposed to be one of the most liberal and progressive countries in the world and still we haven't made our schools safe for kids like him. That something as vital to his future as his education happens in a culture of fear and under the threat of violence.

I reminded myself to be thankful that at least he has what a lot of queer kids don't have: an amazing family behind him. I got an e-mail from his mom yesterday. She thanked me for getting him into camp, saying that he really needed this support, and that he seemed so much more confident and wiser since he came home.

The four days of relative safety and acceptance from his peers really did him some good. Now we just have to get to work on the other 361 days of the year. He still has grade ten to get through. Again.

Let Me Show You

Sometimes I get to go home to Whitehorse for a holiday. I race around for a couple of days trying to visit everyone in the family, and by the time I get back on the plane I am more exhausted than I was before I went on vacation. The last few times I went home were for business. I ran from rehearsals to gigs to interviews, and in my down time I raced around trying to visit everyone in the family. This works best when someone has a birthday or cooks a turkey, then several of us can congregate at one house at the same time. Then I can multitask, visiting four aunts at the same time while simultaneously getting something to eat and waiting for my laundry to dry.

Last spring I went home for the Young Authors' Conference. I spent a couple of days teaching writing in the high school I once attended, was kicked out of, and eventually graduated from. The result was a complicated mix of feelings, the main ingredients being a potent blend of triumph and nausea. I was buying some Advil in the drugstore right after school on the Friday afternoon when I ran into one of my aunts, who had heard a rumour that a couple of my uncles were going to be at the bar shortly after five o'clock that evening. Perfect. I needed a drink.

Turned out that Uncle Rob and Uncle John had had an argument about something a few days earlier, and were still not speaking to one another. The two brothers were sitting at separate tables five feet apart with their backs turned to one another. Small towns and big families. You just learn to work around things. I sat and had a drink with one uncle, then crossed the floor to join the other one. This quickly became ridiculous, so I insisted that they both come outside for a cigarette with me at the same time. My Aunt Cathy, Rob's wife, picked up her purse and came along.

John took a long drag and squinted at me. He had knocked off from work a little early, and had already had a couple. "That a clip-on tie you got on?"

I shook my head. "No way. Double Windsor."

He harrumphed. "That's no double Windsor."

Cathy snorted at her brother-in-law. "What would you know about tying a tie? Last one you wore was at your wedding."

This was a bit of an inside joke. John never got married.

John reached over and pulled my tie undone. "Gimme that thing. I can still tie a perfect double Windsor. The old man showed us all."

He flipped up the collar of his denim work shirt and looped the tie around his neck.

One of the other dudes who had been standing next to us smoking stepped forward, a giant gut bulging behind his navy blue T-shirt, blowing smoke from under the brim of a black leather Caterpillar baseball hat.

"Umm ... mind if I watch? My wife used to tie my ties for me. She passed away three years ago and I haven't been able to dress up since."

This kind of broke my heart. I smiled at him and stepped back so he could join our little circle.

John narrowed a beer-loosened eye at the tie in his hands. Things were not going well. He was drunk, and left-handed. The wide part of the tie was hanging about four inches under his beard. The skinny part was dangling almost at his knees. The label was facing the front, and he had definitely tied some sort of knot, but it wasn't a double, and it wasn't a Windsor.

Cathy shook her head in disgust. "Take that thing off and give it to your niece. Let her show you. Look, we're gathering a crowd here."

It was true. A skinny guy in Carhartt overalls had now stepped up, claiming he was divorced and therefore also needed tie-tying lessons.

I carefully smoothed the tie out on my chest, took a deep breath, and began. "Well guys, first of all you have to start with the right amount of tie on either side ..."

They all leaned forward, fascinated, and watched. When I finished, they all stood back, lit new cigarettes. The guy with the black leather baseball hat cleared his throat.

"So ... you, uh, having a sex change operation or something like that? You wish you were a guy or whatever?"

This is what I like about good old Yukon guys. There is no fumbling around with political correctness. They just blurt shit out.

"No," I say. "I just like to wear men's clothes. I feel more comfortable in them."

This seemed to be enough of an explanation for him, so I stopped there, hoping someone would change the subject. Instead, my Uncle Rob picked up the ball and ran with it.

"Well, you did have that one operation." Rob winked at me. "So everyone would think you were a man? You remember, don't you? You know, that one where they stuck the tube in your ear and sucked out half of your brain?"

The best and most hilarious part came next. Cathy laughed out loud and John choked on his smoke, but the guy with the hat crossed his eyebrows and said "Huh?" like he didn't get it at all.

Which he didn't. Neither did the guy in the overalls. They both stood there, looking confused.

I couldn't write a punch line like that. I laughed so hard I needed to pee. So did my Aunt Cathy.

"Well, gentlemen, if we are finished here, I am going to have to excuse myself. I need to go visit the ladies' room." I swung the old wooden door open for my aunt and left the boys outside. I love those guys. I can still see them there, standing in a circle, with the spring sun still hanging large and low in the sky behind them. The sound of big trucks gearing down on the highway in the background. Talking. Laughing. Smoking.

Good Old Days

I have forty new girlfriends, plus Howard and Warren. I'm leaving Ottawa to move home to East Vancouver as soon as this semester is over, and I'm going to miss all of them a lot. I've been teaching memoir writing to senior citizens, and as I sort through and stow away my favourite memories of my time here, I'm finding that I owe many of them to a small group of grey-haired ladies (and a few gentlemen); their hearts and their wrinkles and their good penmanship.

It used to seem odd to me that a group of mostly women in their sixties and seventies and eighties would get on so well with someone like me, but I have given up questioning why this is and just learned to be thankful for being allowed the opportunity to spend time with them, to encourage them to write down their amazing lives, and to remind them that the history that lives inside their skins is interesting and inspiring and important.

Last semester I had a woman named Catherine in my class. Her stories were poignant and introspective, and run through with a wide-grinned humour and humanity. Everyone in the class loved her. One day about halfway through the semester she stood up and read us a story about what it was like to transition from male to female at her job. What it was like to finally peel back a lifetime of pretending and live truthfully. She told us an amazing account of her co-workers' acceptance and willingness to embrace this new her. No *Well of Loneliness* tale tainted with the taste of hatred; this was a story of tolerance and respect, told with dignity and pride. I had not brought up the kind of obvious question of my gender difference with the class before this, and now I didn't need to. Catherine had taken care of it, reading in a soft but clear voice, her hands shaking only a little bit as she held up her papers and squinted through her bifocals.

The last day of class we had a reading, where everyone could invite a guest or family member to hear a little bit of something they had written during the class, and partake in the complementary dessert trays and tea and coffee. I happened to overhear Warren, my only male student, approach Catherine after the reading was over. Warren was an ex-military man, a boxer in his prime, and a big fan of facts and dates and protocol and order. He thanked Catherine for teaching him to write from his guts, to be brave enough to include an emotion or two in his recounting of events. He shook her hand at first, and then stood back, all of a sudden a little nervous.

"I was wondering if you would mind ... if I might ... if it would be okay with you if I were to give you a hug?" He smiled tentatively at her from under his silver brush cut. Catherine placed her Styrofoam cup on a desk and opened both of her arms.

I can still see the two of them there, she in a respectably long skirt and sweater set, he in his button-down shirt and good dress pants, locked for a few seconds in an awkward and unlikely but heartfelt full body hug. He patted her back with his giant hands, then stepped back to clear his throat, his eyes shining a little.

Last week one of my students was reading the class a story about the day that her lover passed away from pancreatic cancer. The class knew she was a lesbian, but this was the first time she had written openly about her partner. She talked about how they hadn't made love since the diagnosis, how it would have been too painful, literally and figuratively, but how those feelings were still there, that the cancer hadn't destroyed them. She read about bathing her lover well into her illness, and that one day she had leaned over and kissed her clitoris, just to show her that she still loved that part of her, too.

I felt my heart jump into my mouth, and I looked up at the rest of the class to see if there would be any reaction to a real life lesbian uttering one of the c-words in public. Not an eyelash was batted. Except for mine, blinking back tears.

After she finished reading, Hedwig, an eighty-seven-year-old Hungarian woman, spoke first, in a heavy accent.

"Tank you, Hilary, for showing us in words that love is just love." Everyone nodded in agreement, numerous little Kleenex packets were removed from large purses and distributed where needed, and then we moved on.

During the break, one of my students who grew up in Europe during the Second World War brought me a snack.

45

One of those little round Babybel cheeses in the red wax wrapper, a several-times-recycled Ziploc bag full of green grapes with the stems already removed, and a packet of Premium Plus soda crackers.

"Eat, eat," she said, pushing the shopping bag across my desk towards me. "You have had a long day."

She has taken to doing this every week now. I do as I'm told, except for the packet of crackers, which I sneak into my bag when she is not looking and feed to the squirrels in my back yard later. I cannot bring myself to tell a woman who remembers watching the Nazis drive their trucks into her village and take whatever they wanted that I can't eat the crackers she brings me because I am gluten intolerant. It's true. I have fallen in love with every one of them. I even like the sound of their names: Lois, Louise, Mary-Lou, Irene, Dorene, Eleanor, Elsebee, Ghislaine, Hilary, Hedwig, Isabel, Patricia, Margaret, Peg, Joan, Verna, Faith, Kati, and of course Howard and Warren. I know now why we get along so well. We all just love a really good story.

Straighten Up

I try to fit in, I swear I do. Just passing through small-town Northern Ontario, wearing a black parka, driving a silver truck with sensible snow tires, hair shorn recently. Still, the three good old boys smoking cigarettes outside of the only hotel that's still open in town this time of year all stop in mid-sentence to check me out when I walk by. I nod politely, just enough eye contact to not seem suspicious, but not enough that I am looking for a fight. The bells on the door tinkle behind me and the waitress with smoker lady red lips taps the little table in the corner with a plastic-coated menu.

"Right here, hon. Getchoo some coffee?"

I nod. She winks.

I'm getting good at telling, after all these years. No second look. No forced politeness. No clipped words. She thinks I'm a clean-cut young fellow. The old boys outside the front door, I'm not so sure. Maybe they saw a dyke; maybe they think I'm a gay man. There was definitely something about me. Goddamn Fleuvog boots. Have to remember to change into my Sorel snow boots, even though they are a bit hot for the long drives.

I like to think that I am not overly hung up on gender, that I don't treat strangers all that much differently based on the gender I perceive them to be. I also know that this is not quite as true as I might like it to be: my heart pounds faster when I'm alone in the park at night and I think the person walking up behind me is a man, and I would rather buy tampons from a woman.

I do know that there are a lot of people in the world who have a whole lot invested in the man/woman dichotomy, and all of the requisite expectations. I know all this because I have to. I study it all every day. Calling it a survival tactic might be a little dramatic, but it would still be true. So I try to fit in, and most of the time I do. Ironically, for me, not bringing attention to myself means passing just a little bit more as the gender I was raised to call "the other." For the most part, strangers read me as a clean-cut young fellow. But still, if they are looking close enough, there is something about me that doesn't fit. A little gesture, something about my voice, or my hips, or my lips, that makes them take that second, longer, closer look. Some people don't care at all. Some ask if I am in a band, and are we playing in town this weekend. Some just don't like me all that much. And then there are those very few that want to kill me. Whether this is for being an effeminate or homosexual man, or a masculine or queer woman, I am never quite sure. I rarely take the time to ask.

I sit down with my back to the wall. The three good old boys have finished their cigarettes and shuffled back towards their newspaper-strewn table in a rush of chilly smoke-scented air.

"Close the damn door, Albert. I'm not paying to heat all of Ontario." The waitress hustles through the swinging doors with a pot of fresh coffee.

I shudder at the thought of paying the heating bill for this province. Ontario is fucking huge. I know. I just spent the last three days driving across it. I study the menu. Burgers, burgers, and more burgers. What is a gluten intolerant homo in half-hiding to do? What is more gay, ordering a burger without the bun, or just ordering a burger and leaving the bun behind? I could just have a tossed salad, I think, laughing to myself. I'm not going to ask the waitress to find out if the soup of the day is thickened with flour or cornstarch, not with those three guys eyeing me from over by the pinball machine.

"I'll have the breakfast special, please. Over easy. Bacon," I tell her. "No toast," I add, a little under my breath.

Two days later, just outside of Medicine Hat, Alberta, I am letting the little dog run around on the almost winter brown grass outside a rest stop bathroom. I heard the voice before I saw the guy.

"I got a little fella like that in my truck. He a Shih Tzu? Mine's a Cockapoo. You should bring yours over to meet him."

I look up. Late forty-something, grey at the temples, GWG jacket, cowboy boots, bit of a belly, clean-shaven, brass belt buckle, wallet on a chain. Was probably really handsome a few years ago. Still good-looking.

"My wife wanted a little dog. I thought she was nuts, but then I fell in love with the little guy. She got the house. I took the dog."

I nodded. "Mine's a Pekinese-Pomeranian cross."

"Bring him on over to the truck to meet mine." He gestures over his shoulder at a shiny light blue rig winking in the weak sunlight over in the parking lot. He smiles, looks down at my crotch, slowly slides his eyes up over my chest and back to my eyes.

It begins to dawn on me just what he wants to show me back at the rig. It probably isn't his Cockapoo.

"Just got the truck. Bought it off an old-timer who just retired. It's got satellite radio and a flat screen TV in the sleeper. All the amenities." He runs his tongue over his lips.

"I uh ... I like the colour." I bend down and scoop up the little guy, shovel him into the cab of my truck. "Thanks, but I gotta run. Have a good one."

I pull back out onto the highway, under a wide wide sky. Thinking. It could have been the little fluffy dog. Maybe that's what he saw. Or the boots. I had changed back out of the snow boots for my gig in Winnipeg. Goddamn Fleuvogs. Get me every time.

Boner Preservation Society

Last August my sweetheart and I had what we have now taken to calling a speed bump in the road of our love. We broke up for almost two tragic, tear-soaked weeks. When we finally talked about it, we came to the realization that we weren't finished with each other yet. We still wanted to be in some kind of a relationship together; we just didn't want it to look anything like the relationship we had just ended. After extended bouts of painfully honest talking, we emerged with a new game plan. We placed hot raunchy sex at the top of our list of priorities. We decided not to move in together when I returned to Vancouver. We restocked the toy box and signed up for a kinky weekend conference.

Turns out the brand new us model worked so well, we founded a little organization dedicated to keeping the magic alive, complete with a mandate (definitely no pun intended) and mottos and credos and guidelines. Due to both of our travel schedules and propensity for chatting, the Boner Preservation Society now boasts members (pun most certainly intended) all across the continent, a menagerie of like-minded folks of many genders dedicated to conquering bed death of all persuasions. The benefits of BPS membership are so vast and fulfilling that we decided it would be downright selfish to keep them to ourselves, and that in the interests of love and world peace we needed to spread the, umm … word as wide and hard as possible.

So here goes. Imagine a slick looking letterhead and a sturdy, no nonsense font.

The Boner Preservation Society. Our basic motto, in italics, would come right underneath the title: *Feel This.* Right after that will come our mission statement in bold letters: **Putting the cock back in lesbian bed death since 2007.** This will be followed by an explanatory paragraph that states that membership in the BPS is completely free of charge and open to anyone who wishes to preserve the boner, and that boner is a non-gender specific term, as are hard-on, blow job, and ejaculating. These terms are not open for discussion, as long-winded arguments about whether or not female-assigned individuals are capable of wielding boners or getting blow jobs are definite boner killers and are in direct conflict with the official aims of the Boner Preservation Society and are thus forbidden, please see above.

Next will follow the tenets of the BPS, which are malleable and flexible depending on the individual members' tastes and predilections. Members are more than welcome to borrow or extrapolate on ours, but of course it is expected that each of us is ultimately responsible for seeking out, caring for, and maintaining our own individual boners, and as such, the BPS wishes to keep rules regarding the boners of others to a bare minimum, in the interests of boners everywhere, especially as of yet undiscovered techniques or tips. An open mind is a terrible thing to waste.

Some of the tenets and guidelines my sweetheart and I have decided on are:

Want is a need.

Two blocks away is living together.

If you like it shaved, keep it shaved. If you like it plucked, pluck it. If you like it hairy, then take care of it. Don't slack on the personal maintenance. Even if you've been together for twenty years. Make like every date is your first date. She's put up with you for twenty years, the least you can do is bust out the moustache trimmer. Moustache trimmers, of course, are for much more than just moustaches.

Throw out any underwear that is stained, faded to a non-colour, full of holes, or possessing elastic that is no longer interested in its work. Don't argue, just do it. Yes, you do need that new matching bra and panty set or over-priced pair of briefs with the newfangled piping. You do. You probably need a new set of sheets, too. Think you can't afford it? Even 800-thread-count Egyptian cotton will still be cheaper than buying out her half of the Subaru and replacing all the CDs you forgot were hers if she leaves you for her yoga teacher. Think of the big picture. Think of your heart. Think of your boner.

The dog gets his own bed.

Relearn everything you thought you knew about knot-tying.

Foreplay is the new black. Do some research on phero-mones, and when and how they are released, and the men-tal and physical effect of pheromones on arousal, and even love. Pheromones are secreted through the skin as a result of being touched. It's scientific. Someone did a study. I even heard it on the CBC.

Kiss for a minimum of ten seconds at least twice a day. No matter what is going on, or how late for work you are. Involve your tongues. Necking is not optional.

Think of something you have always wanted to try, and try it.

These are a few examples of what works for us. We have found that when actively practicing the tenets of the Boner Preservation Society, the trickier aspects of a healthy rela-tionship somehow become easier. Complex things like inti-macy, honesty, tenderness, and trust are a whole lot easier to get a handle on when you are both sore from all that fucking.

There are things that we have decided are boner kill-ers, but I have chosen not to list them here, mostly because thinking about them kills my boner. Please see above.

There you have it. Membership in the BPS is expanding everyday. We now have a heterosexual caucus and a meno-pause advisory board. We are currently seeking sponsors and are considering developing a crest that can be applied to products and services that are officially recognized by the BPS as boner inducers. So help us spread the word. Find your boner, and love it like it might be your last. Peace be with you. And also with you.

Objects in Mirror Are Queerer Than They Appear

Last month I spent ten days at home in the Yukon, doing research for a new project. I went through as many family photos as I could lay my hands on: sorting through the magic red bag of memorabilia my Aunt Roberta keeps in her basement and sifting through the gigantic mishmash of memories crammed into a box in my mother's guestroom closet. My Grandma Pat won the organization award; hers were some of the only photos actually placed in albums, and each album had a glossary of subjects and decades listed on the inside cover in her bold, confident script. I found a citation for drunk driving from the seventies for one of my uncles, not totally out of character for him, but it was issued at ten o'clock in the morning, which was impressive. I unfolded a stiff and stern letter written by the principal of my father's high school, which would later be my high school, explaining to his parents just why he was going to have to repeat grade ten. It wasn't for lack of intelligence, he made sure to point out. I found a lot of pictures of me as a kid. Way more than I remember anyone taking at the time.

There is the one of me with my dad and my Uncle Rob, who are on either end of a broomstick loaded down with lake trout; I am crouching underneath the fish between the two men, blood spattered up to my elbows, proudly holding up a string of grayling. Me in a campground somewhere up north, exploding out of the willows, carrying a giant log of firewood on my back. Me on the first day of grade one, in a line-up with all the other little girls on the block; all the neighbour girls and my little sister are in sparkly new dresses, their chubby knees scrubbed and squishing out of the tops of sparkling white knee socks. I, on the other hand, am wearing blue corduroys, black rubber boots with red-brown toes, and my Davy Crockett fringed buckskin jacket. Me, in my grade two class photo, front-toothless in a plaid shirt, pearly snaps done right up to my chin, sporting an Andy Gibbish shag do. Me smiling in full hockey gear, lined up with all of my teammates, the only girl in the boy's league.

None of this was surprising to me; I appear to be the same kid I remember being. What I couldn't believe, in retrospect, is that anyone in my family could have actually been surprised when I came out of the closet at eighteen. The evidence was everywhere, right from the start; how could anyone have missed it?

I decided to investigate.

I called up my Aunt Roberta first, because it was almost eight o'clock in the evening, and she goes to bed early. I asked her if she ever suspected that I was gay when I was little, if she ever wondered about the hockey and the buck-skin jackets?

I heard the kitchen chair complain about being dragged across the linoleum, and she sat down.

"I know this sounds silly, but I always just thought you were just who you were. An amazing little strong personality. Thought you got it from your dad."

I asked her if Gran had ever said anything to her about me and the gay.

"Gran's gone to bed already, but I do remember her saying to me that you were exactly right. All you kids turned out to be exactly who God meant you to be. I mean, you can call her in the morning if you want to, but I know that's what she'll say."

My grandma Pat was good for an awesome quote, as usual.

"I never labeled you as anything. You were just boyish, and you did boyish things. Keep in mind that we just didn't think like that back then, you see. Any knowledge of homosexuality I might have had would have gone back to Victorian times. All those novels. You probably skirted under my radar, because you weren't wearing hoop skirts and high button boots."

My mom swore she had no clue whatsoever. "My mind never went there. I just let you be what you wanted to be. Not very helpful, I guess. I'm sorry."

My Aunt Cathy echoed my mom. "I just thought you were a little brat because you refused to wear a dress to our wedding."

My Aunt Norah thought my sister and I were just polar opposites, that was all. "Carrie was the prissy little girl, and you ... weren't. You were just your own little people. When you were in your teens I remember thinking ... knowing somehow that you weren't happy, you just seemed tense inside your own skin. I knew there was something going on with you, but I didn't know what it was. We didn't have to have a label for everything back then."

My Uncle John was cooking an omelet in the background when I talked to him. "Sorry, kiddo, but I can't identify the moment we realized you had gone to the dark side. We were just glad you weren't stupid. There's no cure for stupid. There was that one time, you were only six or so, when you gave me supreme shit for not attending to my fishing rod, but I don't think that had much to do with your sexuality."

My Uncle Rob was pensive, thinking over his response a bit before speaking. "Well ... you can see why we wouldn't have thought much about it. There's lots of hetero butch chicks out there, to be honest. Especially up here."

"On the other hand," he continued, "maybe a guy should have twigged due to your aversion to wearing a dress, but who cares, anyway? I've always said, it's your soap and your dick, and you can wash it as fast as you want."

So it appears that for all those years, in all those photographs of that little tomboy, there was only one member of my family wondering about me.

And that was me.

Truth Story

A couple of years ago I was backstage at a little music festival with my friend and guitar player, Richard. It was a breezy blue-skied July day, drawing quite a decent crowd for a small town. I pulled back the velvet curtain a crack to have a sneak peek at our audience. The entire first row was a beefy, bleeding tattooed wall of biker-looking types. I swallowed and pulled the curtain back.

"Rico ..." I whispered. "I think we're gonna have to change up our set a little. I think maybe we need to drop the Francis story and do the fishing story instead."

The Francis story was a tale about a little boy who liked to wear dresses. I thought maybe a less faggy, more fishing-oriented piece might go over a little better with this crowd.

Richard took a deep breath and gave me his I-am-about-to-tell-you-something-for-your-own-good look.

"First of all," he began, "the truck is parked right backstage. Second, artists are always allowed to talk about shit that other people would get punched out for bringing up, remember? It's part of the deal."

I nodded, because this was true. Richard inhaled again,

obviously not finished yet.

"But most important of all is, don't be a chickenshit, Coyote. Have some balls. What, you only going to tell that story to people who don't need to hear it?"

"You fucker." I smiled at him.

He shrugged. He knew me. Knew what to say to activate my stubborn streak.

The biggest and most bad-assed-looking of the bikers stood there in the front row, his veiny forearms crossed over his black T-shirt, for the first ten minutes of my set. He even laughed here and there, the skin around his eyes crinkling into well-worn crow's feet every time he smiled. I started to relax a little, and when I started the first couple of lines of the Francis story, Richard tipped his head in my direction in approval and played like an angel beside me.

Halfway through the story, I watched the gigantic man in the front row start to unpeel himself right in front of me. First he uncrossed his arms and let them fall to his sides. Then he bit his lower lip, and his handlebar moustache began to quiver a little. By the end, he was crying giant man-sized tears, unabashedly letting them roll down his dusty cheeks and disappear into his beard. He almost got me choked up too, just watching him. I was used to the drag queens losing it in the last couple of paragraphs of the Francis story, but this was something else altogether.

After, when Richard and I were loading gear into the back of his pick-up, I looked up and he was standing next to the table that held the cheese trays and the juice cooler, waiting to talk to me.

He rushed up and picked me right up off the ground in a cigar-scented hug. When he let me back down to the ground, he still held both of my hands in his baseball glove-sized hands, squeezing them until it almost hurt.

"I just had to thank you. Just had to tell you how much that story you told meant to me." He pulled me up close to him, and lowered his voice a couple of decibels. "My baby brother James died from AIDS, ten years ago tomorrow. My only brother. I loved him like crazy when we were kids, but my dad … well … let's just say the old man wasn't very flexible in his beliefs about certain things. He never understood Jamie, right from the get-go, and Christ, he was hard on the kid. Beat the living shit out of him one time when he caught him wearing my sister Donna's lipstick. Finally kicked him out when Jamie was fifteen. Nobody knew, back then, and by the time we did, it was too late. I never stuck up for him, never said a word, and to this day I have never forgiven myself for it. My baby brother, out on the street. How else was he going to get by? He was only a fucking kid."

He looked me right in the eyes. By this time, both of us were crying.

"He was the sweetest fucking kid in the world. Your little friend in that story reminded me of James. There were five of us kids, but he was always my mom's favourite. The old man blamed her, said she babied him, but we all knew he was just born like that. That was just who he always was." He cleared his throat and wiped his eyes on the hair on the back of his hands. Looked a bit sheepish all of a sudden. "Anyways, just wanted to thank you for that. Good stuff."

Then he shook my hand and was gone. I've never forgotten him, and I imagine him standing behind me whenever I find myself scared of the next story I am about to tell, or afraid of the people I'm about to tell it to.

Last week I walked into a classroom at the college in Powell River, to tell stories to a bunch of Adult Education students. Working-class town, working-class guys all lined up in the back row. I found myself wishing with my whole heart I had not chosen to wear a paisley dress shirt that morning. What was I thinking?

Then I took a deep breath and told them a story. I started with the one about my dad. The one where I had almost given up wishing he would quit drinking, but then one day he did. Afterward, this guy with biceps the size of my thighs came up and thanked me. He had sleeve tattoos and could barely squeeze his muscles into his white Stanfield crewneck.

"I really liked the one about your dad," he explained. "I could totally relate to him. I used to be a welder, too."

Gifted

I finally got my stuff out of storage and went through it all. There was the usual garbage bag full of clothes I wouldn't wear again and didn't miss, and I bundled them all up to donate them.

It was one of those days: take out the recycling, pay the bills, mail stuff, buy dish soap, drop off the old clothes. I took the little dog with me. He is friendly, and I am prone to chatting up strangers, so it wasn't unusual when halfway up the block the lady bent down to pet the dog and the two of us got to talking.

"He's so sweet, and friendly."

I nodded proudly. He is. He had flopped his head over her bent knee, and was reaching for her hand with his face.

"It's like he can tell I was having a shitty day. That I needed a bit of love."

This was all I needed.

"Actually," I told her, puffing up a little, "he is a gifted therapeutic pet."

He blinked at her with his watery brown eyes. I continued.

"My puppy-sitter takes him to visit her father with Alzheimer's. That's how we found out about his natural ability to comfort the sick. And then he started visiting her mom, who has since passed away. The nurses take him around to visit the other patients. They say he's better than the trained animals that come in. He was always good at knowing when someone wasn't feeling very well. He's extra sweet if you are sick."

He had his forehead pressed into her thigh now, his tail wagging slowly, the rest of him motionless.

The woman raised her face up at me, and that was the first time I really looked at her. Her hair was cropped close to her scalp, and she had amazingly beautiful big eyes, which were shining full of tears. She let out a long breath.

"You should take him into the cancer ward. They would love him there. He really is a special guy. They could use him there. I should know." Her eyes met mine. "I've just come through my third battle with cancer myself."

I knew I had seen that hair cut before. My friend Carole from Ottawa, most recently. The short short hair of a woman who recently had none at all. Not short hair like mine. Short hair like hers. Short hair that her girlfriends try to tell her just makes her look younger, like a supermodel, or that gymnast in the seventies, what was her name again? Short hair that is growing in a different colour, so much more wiry, or curlier than her hair used to be, before all … this.

I didn't say much, just mumbled something awkward around the lump in my throat.

She stood up, wiping her hands on her slacks. Then she pulled a giant ring of keys out of her handbag and opened the trunk of her car. She hauled out a vacuum cleaner and turned again to grab milk crate full of cleaning supplies. I stumbled over the dog's leash to help her with the crate, but she beat me to it. Pine Sol, ammonia, bleach, Pledge, Windex, stuff like that.

"You moving in here?" I motioned to the empty house on the other side of the hedge that bordered the sidewalk where we were standing.

She shook her head. "I run a housecleaning business. The real estate agent hired me to do this one."

She exhaled and dropped the crate of cleaning supplies next to my boots, then turned to grab a Home Depot bag full of what looked like paper towels and rags. I looked down at all those chemicals.

"You're back at work already?" It sounded stupid, even leaving my lips.

She smiled, shrugged a little. "A girl's gotta work. Cancer doesn't care about who pays the rent."

The little dog was wagging around her feet now, flipping his ears back like he does, looking for some more pats. I pulled on the leash so she didn't trip over him. I told her it was nice to talk to her, wished her best of luck.

We exchanged a few more niceties, told each other to have good days, then she bent down to pick up her vacuum cleaner. I got about ten steps down the sidewalk before I stopped and turned.

"You wouldn't happen to know anyone who needs some

clothes, would you? They're all clean and in good condition."

Her eyes glanced up and down my frame. "They would probably be too big for me."

"They're all men's clothes," I told her. "Shirts and ties and stuff. I just thought maybe you might know someone who could use them."

Her eyes lit up. "Someone like my nineteen-year-old transgendered son?" She reached out her thin arm to take the bag from me.

I smiled wide. "Yeah, someone just like that."

She opened the bag, and closed it again. "He just came out to me recently. He will love this. We can't afford a whole new wardrobe right now."

"Tell him someone named Ivan Coyote gave them to him."

"I thought that was you." She was beaming now. "He loves your books. I didn't ask because I didn't want to seem weird."

I didn't hug her because I didn't want to seem weird, I thought, but said nothing.

"Tell him hello for me. I'm not sure if any of them are cool enough for a nineteen-year-old, but tell him hey for me anyways."

"It was a pleasure to meet you." She started to shake my hand, and then pulled me into a stiff, awkward hug. She smelled like something vaguely lavender. "You take good care of yourself."

"You too. You take care."

Me and the little dog left her there, dragging her cleaning stuff up the stairs of the refurbished heritage house that wasn't hers. There was so much I wanted to say to her, but I couldn't speak.

So I wrote it down.

Talking to Strangers

I was on tour again, just landed in Calgary, and more than a little jetlagged. I heaved my suitcase into the trunk of the cab and slid into the back without even looking at the driver. I laid my head on the leather seat and closed my eyes, which were burning and felt like they had sawdust in them.

"Beautiful day today, right?" the driver broke the silence. His voice was soft and syrupy, supple.

I sighed and opened my eyes. He was right. It really was a beautiful spring day on the prairies. I hadn't even noticed. I sat up and passed him the printed out e-mail with the name and address of the hotel on it. He reached over his shoulder into the backseat, and when he gently took the paper, I noticed his hands. His fingers were remarkably long and slender, poised like praying mantises. His nails were a little bit too long, and buffed to a high gloss. They almost looked like they had a coat of clear polish on them. Gold pinky ring with a sapphire in it. I'm not one for stereotypes, but the man had gay hands. I followed his gay hands up his arms and found his face in the rear-view mirror. His facial hair was immaculately trimmed, and his eyes sparkled velvet and brown from under caterpillar eyelashes. Handsome fellow. His eyes met mine and he raised one eyebrow, almost flirting.

"You travelling alone?"

I nodded. We exchanged the usual: no, I didn't live here, yes, I was here on business. He was almost finished for the day, he had started at four a.m., no, he didn't mind the long days, it left him time to study at night and take classes, University of Alberta, kinesiology. That kind of thing.

Then he cleared his throat. Asked me if I was married. I told him no. His eyes caught mine again in the rear-view mirror for a little too long, and he squinted at me for a second, like he was pondering something unsaid.

"Can I ask you something personal? Something I've always wondered about you people?"

I shrugged a bit, told him sure, he could ask, but I couldn't speak for all of us, I was only the one person, couldn't really speak for the many. I wasn't quite sure if he thought I was a dyke, or if he was asking me to comment on behalf of gay men everywhere, but I figured the answer to this query might be found in his question, so I told him go ahead, ask, and I would try to answer.

"Do you live alone?"

I told him yes, I did.

"Don't you love your family?"

"Of course," I told him. "But most of them live up north. I need to live here, in a bigger city, for work."

"I live with my brother," he nodded firmly. "And his wife and their two sons. Also the mother of my brother's wife, and her sister, the great-aunt, I think you call it in English. It is very good for all of us. Especially my nephews. No daycare. My brother drives this taxi cab nights. And I am learning from the children how to be a father to my own."

I nodded, and then asked the obvious. Was he married? He couldn't have been older than twenty-five or so, and was kind of obviously at least a little bit gay, but it seemed like the polite thing to ask.

"My parents have arranged for me to be married in Pakistan this August. I will fly over and my wife will return to Canada with me."

"Your fiancée lives in Pakistan? Do you get to see her much? That must be hard."

He shook his head, smiling. "I haven't seen her since we were four years old. But my mother sends me pictures. She is a very beautiful girl."

"Do you love her?"

"She is a very beautiful girl," he repeated.

I nodded. He was trying to understand my lifestyle, so the least I could do was return the courtesy.

He took another deep breath. "So, forgive me if this is a rude question, but don't you think living alone without any family is a little bit selfish? And don't you ever get lonely?"

"I get home to the North at least twice a year, sometimes more, and I talk on the phone to everyone all the time. In fact, I just talked to my grandmother for an hour while I was waiting for the plane in Ottawa. And yes, maybe living alone is a little bit selfish, but I'm a writer and work at home, and I need the solitude to get any work done."

He nodded. "Your people, I've noticed, are often very creative. I get a lot of movie people in my taxi cab these days, one time a very big star. Fancy guy. Big tipper. Why are you all so creative?"

Again I told him that I couldn't really speak for all of us, that I was only one person, and I wasn't sure that there were any more creative types among us per capita than any other segment of the population, maybe just those of us he noticed, blah blah blah. He didn't seem convinced by my half-assedly politically correct argument.

The cab pulled up in front of my hotel, and a gust of wind twirled a mini-cyclone of dust and bits of trash across the road in front of us.

He shivered a bit in the wind, wearing only a deep blue dress shirt. He gingerly placed my suitcase on the sidewalk, and turned to shake my hand. His palms were almost un-naturally soft. I thought about his wife. I thought about him. He blinked a few times, his giant eyelashes dusting his pretty boy cheeks.

"I want to thank you sincerely for answering all my questions. I hope you didn't find me too rude. I've never met one of you that I felt I could ask before this, but you have very kind eyes, and I've always wondered these things about you people. About you white people."

The Rest of Us

I got the call on a Sunday night. My gran was in the hospital, and the doctor had advised the family that it was time.
Time to call everybody home.

I arrived bleary-eyed at the Whitehorse airport the next
day. My mom and Aunt Nora were both there to meet me
and my cousin Robert and his girlfriend. They looked so
tired and worried; the skeleton was showing behind their
faces, their eyes red-rimmed and puffy. They took us directly to the hospital, our suitcases stowed away in the trunk of
the car.

I knew my gran wasn't going to look good, and I thought
I had steeled myself for the worst. Still, my heart stopped
and dropped when I laid my eyes on the tiny shape of her,
the outline of her hips and legs barely visible under the
green sheets and blanket. Impossibly frail and little. Almost
gone already, it seemed. I had promised myself I would be
strong for my mom, that I wasn't going to cry. So much for
that.

"Talk to her," my Uncle Dave said, waving two fingers at
Robert and me. "The nurses say she can still hear us."

And so we did. All afternoon we sat and talked. To her,

to each other. Remember her bad cooking? Baloney roast? Boiled hamburger? Lemon hard cake, cousin Dan had dubbed her attempt at meringue. How she loved us all, no matter who we were, no matter what we did. I volunteered for night shift, and sat next to the laboured breathing shape of her with my two uncles, whispering stories through the dark to each other, into her ear, slipping our warm hands under the covers to grasp her limp, cold ones.

By early the next afternoon all of us were there. Five of her children, eight grandchildren, plus partners. I began to worry that we were pissing the nursing staff off a little, them trying to work around us, asking us to leave the room so they could change her sheets. Ten or fifteen of us at a time, filing like exhausted soldiers out into the hallway to stand around, teary-eyed and sometimes bickering. I asked one of the nurses if we were driving anyone nuts yet, wasn't it hard trying to do her job with the whole lot of us underfoot? She shook her head and said no, that the First Nations people had taught the nursing staff what an extended family could really look like, and that it is often easier when the family is there to help keep an eye on a patient. She said that what was really hard was when someone was dying without anyone there at all. This choked me up a little, and she shoved a no-name box of Kleenex across the counter at me with a latex-gloved hand. She had said it out loud. The doctor was kind, and had talked around it. Don't get your hopes up, she had said. We are keeping her comfortable, the doctor said. The doctor didn't lie, but it was the nurse who actually said the words. My grandmother was dying.

Florence Amelia Mary Lawless Daws passed away a little after eleven a.m. on May 13, surrounded by seventeen members of her family. Our hands made a circle, all touching her tiny body as her chest rose and fell, and then stopped. I hesitate to say her death was beautiful, because it means I have to miss her now, but it was.

My family asked me to write and read her eulogy. Blessing from the family, the Catholics now call it. I call it what it is. Of course I said yes, I would be honoured, and I was.

I wrote about the values the tiny little Cockney/Irish/ Roma woman had lived and died by, and raised us all up to believe in. Love your family, work hard, save your money, have faith, and be grateful for what you have. I worked really hard on the eulogy. I wanted to do justice to her memory, to honour everything she was. There were over four hundred people at the service, and not a dry eye among them when I was finished.

Up at the graveyard, after the internment, I hugged strangers and shook hands. Suddenly I found myself surrounded by Catholic priests. They were being uncommonly nice to me, the queer granddaughter in the shirt and tie. Maybe they make special allowances in the case of a death in the family, I thought. Or maybe they were still hoping to save my soul. The bishop hugged me, and then held both of my hands in his too-soft ones.

"Excellent job, young man. Your grandmother would have been very proud of you today, son. Strong work, young fellow."

My mother heard him too. I saw her freeze. Waiting.

"Thank you, Father," I said. That was why he seemed to like me so much. He didn't know who I really was.

The bishop caught up with me again at the reception, back at the funeral home. We were both leaned over the cheese platters, when he addressed me a second time.

"Once again, I must say, you are a gifted orator. A natural, even. Have you ever considered the priesthood?"

This time it was my Aunt Nora within direct earshot, and she stopped in mid-bite, half a baby carrot removed from her mouth and dropped on a small paper plate. Her eyes met mine, and she tried not to wince.

I took a deep breath. Thought about my beloved gran, about how much she loved the Church, and respected the bishop. He seemed like a nice enough guy.

I'm not going to lie and say that one hundred wise-ass quips didn't run through my head and gather on my tongue. They did. But what counts is what I actually said.

"No Father, I have to admit, I have never considered the priesthood. But thank you again for the compliment."

The bishop nodded, and everyone around us relaxed and resumed eating and talking.

I like to think my gran would have been real proud of me.

A Butch Roadmap

A while ago, I came upon an article in the online version of the LGBT newspaper *Xtra!* entitled "Winnipeg Pride wants parade to be 'family friendly.'" In it, the then-chair of the previous year's pride parade was quoted as saying, "We have to remember that this is a public event; part of the parade is to show people we're not extremists." When pressed to explain just what she meant by extremists, she responded, "Drag queens and butch women." She then added it was important to show the people of Winnipeg that there are "mainstream" queer community members, too, like "lawyers and doctors."

I was so mad, I seriously considered a stern letter. The subtext of her words stung my eyes and burned in my throat. Apparently, according to this genius, regardless of my politics or attitude or tactics, I was an extremist, by virtue only of my appearance. Nothing of who I was or what I might contribute to my community mattered, because of what I looked like. In order to be acceptable to the good citizens of Winnipeg, we needed to put forward a more "mainstream" face to the general public, liberally laced with professionals. I wondered how this line of reasoning was going to go

over with the many perverted transsexual leatherdyke lawyers from working-class backgrounds I am lucky enough to
know. Apparently this woman hadn't read that part of queer
history where drag queens and butches started the whole
thing, by finally standing up and rioting in response to po-
lice persecution and brutality. And now she didn't want us
at her parade anymore. We weren't family friendly enough.
Then I wondered what exactly this meant for those of us
with families.

Then recently, I heard a rumour that the younger
queers don't like the word butch. This makes me wonder:
if I were twenty years old right now instead of forty, what
would I call myself?

I grew up without a roadmap to myself. Nobody taught
me how to be a butch. I didn't even hear the word until I
was twenty years old. I first became something I had no
name for in solitude, and only later discovered the word for
what I was, and realized there were others like me. So now I
am writing myself down, sketching directions so that I can
be found, or followed.

If the word for you is butch, remember this word. It will
be used against you.

If the word for you is butch, remember. Remember that
your history is one of strength and survival, and largely silent. Do not hide this word under your tongue. Do not whisper it, or sweep it under the basement stairs. Let it fill up
your chest, and widen your shoulders. Wear it like a sleeve
tattoo, like a medal of valour.

Learn to recognize other butches for what they really

are: your people. Your brothers, or sisters. Both are just words that mean family. Other butches are not your competition, they are your comrades. Be there when they need you. Go fishing together. Help each other move. Polish your rims or your chrome or your boots or your knobs together. See these acts for what they really are: solidarity.

Do not give your butch friend a hard time about having a ponytail, a Pomeranian, nail polish, or even a smart car. Get over yourself. You are a rare species, not a sterotype.

Trim your nails short enough that you could safely insert your fingers into your own vagina, should you ever want to.

Scars and purple thumbnails are a status symbol. When attempting to operate, maintain, or repair anything mechanical, always remember the words of my grandmother: "The vast majority of machines are still designed, built, driven, and fixed by men. Therefore, they cannot be that complicated."

Be exceptionally nice to old ladies. They really need their faith in the youth of today restored. Let them butt in line at the grocery store. Slow down and walk with them at crosswalks so they're not the only ones holding up traffic. Drive your grandma to bingo. Shovel her driveway. Let chivalry live on.

If you're going to be the kind of butch who is often read as a man or a boy, then be the kind of man or boy you wish you would have slept with in high school. Be a gentleman. Let her finish her sentence. Share the armrest. Do her laundry without shrinking anything this time. Buy her her very own cordless drill.

Open doors for men, saying, "Let me get that for you."

Carry a pocket knife, a lighter, and a handkerchief on your person at all times. Learn flashy lighter tricks, how to tie a half hitch, a slip knot, and a double Windsor.

Learn how to start a fire with a flint and some dry moss. Then use lighter fluid or gasoline, and a blowtorch. Burn most of your eyebrows off lighting the barbecue with a birthday candle, and then tell everybody all about it.

Wear footwear that makes a clomping sound, as opposed to a tick or a swish.

Let the weird hairs on your chin and around your nipples grow unhindered.

Learn how to knit, quilt, crochet, or hook rugs: women appreciate a fellow who isn't afraid of their feminine side.

Practice saying you're sorry. This is one activity where you should not use your father as a role model. Fonzie was an asshole. If you are too young to remember who the Fonz was, then YouTube it.

Locker room talk? A sure-fire way not to get laid a second time.

Learn to recognize other butches for who they really are: your people. Your brothers, or your sisters. Both are just words that mean family.

Hats Off

To all the beautiful, kick-ass, fierce, and full-bodied femmes out there, I would like to extend my thanks to you. It is for you that I press my shirts and carefully iron my ties. It is for you that I make sure my underwear and socks match. It is to you that I tip my cowboy hat. It is for you that I polish my big black boots.

I know that sometimes you feel like nobody truly sees you. I want you to know that I see you. I see you on the street, on the bus, in the gym, in the park. I don't know why I can tell that you are not straight, but I can. Maybe it is the way you look at me. Please don't stop looking at me the way you do. All of my life I have been told that I am ugly, I am less than, I am not a man, I am unwanted. Until you came along, I believed them. Please do not ever stop looking at me the way you do.

I would never say that the world is harder on me than it is you. Sometimes you are invisible. I have no idea what this must feel like, to pass right by your people and not be recognized. To not be seen. I cannot hide, unless I am seen as something I am not. This is not more difficult, it is just different.

I know those shoes are fucking killing your feet. I want you to know how much I appreciate that you are still wearing them. You look hot. I love you in them. They look great with that dress. If it makes you feel any better at all, the boots I have on right now weigh approximately twelve pounds apiece and they make the soles of my feet burn like diaper rash in a heat wave and it feels like I'm wearing ski boots when I have to walk up stairs. But I wear them for you. Even still, my new boots are velvet slippers compared to your knee-high five-inch heels. I notice, and I salute you.

I promise, I am not just staring at your tits. I am trying to look you directly in the eyes, but you are almost eight inches taller than me, please see above note regarding your five-inch heels. At the same time, I would like to mention that while I was trying to look you in the eyes, I couldn't help but notice your lovely new pendant. I am sure it really brings out the colour of your eyes, if I could see them.

I want to thank you for coming out of the closet. Again and again, over and over, for the rest of your life. At school, at work, at your kid's daycare, at your brother's wedding, at the doctor's office. Thank you for sideswiping their stereotypes. I never get the chance to come out of the closet, because my closet was always made of glass. But you do it for me. You fight homophobia in a way that I never could. Some of them think I am queer because I am undesirable. You prove to them that being queer is your desire.

Thank you for loving me because of who I am and what I look like, not in spite of who I am and what I look like.

Thank you for smelling so good.

Thank you for holding my hand on the sidewalk during the hockey playoffs. I know it is probably small-minded of me to smile wickedly at all the drunken dudes in jerseys smoking outside the sports bar in between periods because you are so fucking hot, and you are with me and not them, but I can't help it. That's right, fellas. You want her but she wants me. How do you like them apples?

Thank you for wearing matching bra and panties. I don't know why this makes my life seem so perfect, but it really does.

Thank you for reaching out in the dark at the movie theatre to grab my hand during the scary parts. It makes me feel like I am strong, that I can take care of you. Even if there is no such thing as vampires, and you do so much yoga that you could probably easily kick my ass.

I want you to know I love your crooked tooth, your stretch marks, the missing part of your finger, your short leg, your third nipple, your lazy eye, your cowlick, your birthmark shaped like Texas. I love it all.

I want you to know that I know it is not always easy to love me. That sometimes my chest is a field full of landmines and where you went last night you can't go tomorrow. There is no manual, no street map, no helpline you can call. My body does not come with instructions, and sometimes even I don't know what to do with it. This cannot be easy, but still, you touch me anyway.

Thank you for escorting me into the women's washroom because the floor of the men's was covered in something unmentionable. Thank you for asking me if I had a

tampon in my purse so loudly that the lady in the turquoise
sweatshirt did a double take before gathering up her daughter and hitting me with a pool noodle. I can't say for sure
whether that is what actually would have happened, but
thanks to you, I didn't have to find out.

Thank you for wearing that dress just because you
knew it would match my shirt. Together, we are unstoppable. When seen through your eyes, I am beautiful. Turns
out I was a swan the whole time.

Straight Teens Talk Queer

Recently I had the pleasure of being a teen mentor for a group of nine youth at the Vancouver Public Library's annual book camp. My kids were almost frighteningly smart, and savvy, and hilarious, and of course, well-read.

I decided I was going to put all that intelligence and potential and Internet virtuosity to work and get them to write my column for me this month. We set out to write a piece about homophobia from the point of view of a group of predominantly heterosexual youth. As they were a rather studious lot, we started off by not only defining homophobia for the reader, but by including a historical overview of how definitions of the word homophobia might have changed over the years. Turns out that in 1958, there was no such word as homophobia listed in the Comprehensive Word Guide; all the kids could find was a definition of homosexuality listed under "certain specific sexual aberrations, perversions, abnormal practices, etc." alongside thirty-nine other practices which included bestiality, auto-fellatio, cunnilingus, and coprolagnia, which none of us had ever heard of, but we looked it up. Look it up. I dare you.

We all found it notable that a mere fifty years later, Webster's defined homophobia as "the fear of or contempt for lesbians and gay men, or behavior based on such a feeling."

We then came up with a list of questions, and everybody took them home for homework. This was followed the next day by a rather raucous and ridiculously funny discussion resulting in all of us being resoundingly shushed twice, because we were, after all, in a library. Here is a list of the questions and a sampling of their answers.

Do you think that homophobia still exists in our society?

Sarah, age sixteen: It may not be as harsh as it was in the past, but it is still there. People in the gay community are not always beaten for being who they are but they are definitely not always welcomed by all the people around them.

Wednesday, seventeen: Being a high school student myself I can safely say yes, it does. I do believe that acceptance is a lot more common than it was twenty, or even ten years ago. Things are definitely looking up. I see straight boys with their arms around each other as a sign of affection, I see boys wearing pink and not getting called the F word. I see girls holding hands and no one is writing accusatory labels on their lockers.

Why do you think homophobia still exists?

Megan, sixteen: I blame religion, or, more accurately, religious fanatics.

Sarah: Not all cultures suppressed it for thousands of years. In Greece they used to wrestle naked. That's how the Olympics got started.

Olivia, fifteen: People prefer the ordinary.

Annalise, fifteen: Some people are closed-minded and not accepting of what is different and strange to them.

Kylee, seventeen: It's all Adam and Eve stuff. People are afraid that if they allow it to happen God will be angry and bring damnation or something down upon them.

Wednesday: I'm not sure that there is only one thing or person to blame, unless you can blame the entire human race and call it a night. But that won't bring back the numerous suicides, and it won't make things any better.

Julian, fifteen: Some bigotry is rooted deeper than just in ignorance, but hopefully those people will eventually succumb to the inevitable and keep their mouths shut.

Do you want to end homophobia, if indeed you feel it still exists? Why?

Sarah: Of course I want it to end.

Neil, seventeen: Why should straight people care? Why do white people care that we are mean to black people? It's a moral issue and we have accepted that it is not okay to discriminate ... period.

Does homophobia impact your life in any way, or anyone who you know or care about?

Sarah: One of my best friends felt so afraid of what would happen to him in my town that he felt the need to move. I haven't seen him in over two years.

Lisa, sixteen: I've grown up in a family that says they

find nothing wrong with it, but have some serious issues, and I feel embarrassed. I meet these truly interesting and inspiring people, and it hurts to learn that they have been treated wrongly, especially when I hear the slander coming from the mouths of people I respect and trust. What if, somewhere down the line, I realize that I'm not heterosexual? I won't have a problem with it, but what of my friends and family? Will they be supportive or turn their backs?

Give an example of ways we could change things.

Sarah: My school tries to stop people from using the term gay in a derogatory fashion by making the student who uses the word write a 5,000-word essay on why the use of that word could be offensive. But I don't think this works because it is hardly ever done or checked up on.

Julian: The fact that Gay/Straight Alliance groups can exist is a sign of the times. Fifty years ago, such groups would have been counterproductive: instead of a safe place, these groups would have been bull's-eyes.

Annalise: Set an example of not being homophobic, and not making homophobic remarks, and hope that others take on that acceptance too.

Megan: My school has a program on sexual orientation; they mix it in with sex ed and suicide awareness. The leaders asked us what we would do if we found out one of our friends were gay. If you were okay, you went to one side of the room; if you weren't, you went to the other side of the room. Only one person stayed on the not okay side.

So. There you have it. I think there is only one right

thing to do with our society. We have to turn it over to these people. Which is great, because eventually this is going to happen anyway, whether the rest of us are ready for it or not.

Some of My Best Friends Are Rednecks

A friend of mine stopped me in the street the other day to tell me a story. This is not uncommon; in fact, I consider random story stoppings to be a job benefit, kind of like healthcare for storytellers, or at least heartcare. Except I didn't like the story he told me. Didn't like it at all.

I guess I should start by describing what this friend looks like, not because it matters at all to me, but because it matters to the story. My friend has long brown hair and a kind of bushy beard. He is from a working-class coal mining town in the southern US. He looks like a bit like a good old boy. Like a redneck straight white guy, to use his words, not mine.

He had been riding the good old Number 20 Victoria bus downtown a couple of days ago, reading a book. To be more specific, because it matters to this story, he was reading one of my books. As in a book I wrote, not just one I owned and then lent to him.

So he notices kind of by accident that there is a young woman sitting right across from him, in those seats that face each other at the back of the bus, and she is glaring at him. Staring and glaring. He ignores her for a bit, hoping she will just go away, or decide to stare at someone else, but she just keeps right on, laying the old stink eye on him.

Finally she breaks the silence. She asks him why he is reading that book.

He tells her because he likes to read.

The exchange that ensued goes something like this:

"Do you know the author of that book is a lesbian? Why would someone like you want to read a lesbian book? What is in it for you?"

I should mention at this point—not that it really mattered to my friend or myself, but the story requires it—that this young woman had short hair and was dressed, well, kind of dykey. Not that one should assume anything about a perfect stranger, but it is important for the narrative here that we all understand that my friend figured it was more likely that she was taking issue with his choice of reading material for some sort of political reasons stemming from the fact that she was queer herself, rather than her being a right-wing evangelical Christian who objected to apparent straight guys reading queer books on public transit for religious reasons. Just so we've got that part straight, at least.

So my friend answers her.

"Well, I am reading it first of all because I like the writing, and second it is funny, and if I am getting what you are getting at here, then yes, I am reading a book written by a lesbian because I am learning something from it, and it challenges me. Isn't that a good thing, that a straight guy can read a queer book in broad daylight on a city bus without even thinking about it? Because I didn't think about it at all, until you brought it up. I mean, isn't that the kind of world we are all wishing for?"

But she was like a dog after a bone.

"It challenges you?"

"Yeah, it makes me think about stuff in a different way. Also, Ivan is a friend of mine."

She snorts. "Oh, of course. Ivan is a friend of yours."

This is where my buddy started to feel a little defensive. They trade a few more clipped sentences. Then she says:

"Oh, now you're going to get all angry at me. How typically male of you."

The conversation continued to swirl around the drain like that for a short while, and finally my friend realized this was a discussion he was biologically predestined to never win, so he went back to reading his book. Or should I say, my book? He bought it with his own money.

My friend and I had a lengthy caffeine-fueled discussion about it all later that afternoon. The first thing I felt when he told me this story was shame. Shame for my people. Shame that she slid herself so seamlessly into the stereotypical shell of the man-hating lesbian and harassed a perfect stranger on the bus, backhandedly in my name.

He reminded me that we had no way of knowing the kind of pain or suffering that the young woman might have survived at the hands of men that looked just like him. He reminded me that even though she pissed him off and he walked away feeling defensive and ruffled, he never once felt unsafe, and that we might not be able to say the same thing for her. I feel it is important to the narrative here to stress again that it was he who reminded me of these things, not the other way around.

And it got me to thinking. I was reminded of a discussion I had recently with a femme friend of mine who is the coordinator of a women's centre at a university, and every September she does orientations for the new students, of all genders. She tells all the young men that she assumes that they are her allies in the fight against sexism. That she assumes they are on her side and there to help her change the world, until proven otherwise. She tells me she loves to watch them raise their heads and straighten their shoulders. She loves to watch the young women too, as it washes across their faces that they can be real feminists and fight sexism and get to keep their boyfriends if they want to; it doesn't make them any less a part of the sisterhood.

 · What a powerful thought. To assume that the stranger on the bus is on your side, until he (or she) proves that they are not. To drop the gloves and turn the boxing ring into a place to talk and listen to each other, instead of using the winds of change to fan the flames of conflict. I was reminded of this last week by a friend of mine. Remember him? He kind of looks like a redneck. But he is not.

One Among the Many

The room smelled like hair wax and Old Spice deodorant and cigarette smoke caught in clothes. There was the clunk of shit-kicker boots and the creak of leather jackets and talking. Always there was talking. I was in the conference room of a hotel in downtown Oakland, at the first ever Butch Voices conference, billed as "four days of workshops, entertainment and bonding for butches, aggressives, studs, and allies." It was the first time in my life I had ever been in a room surrounded by people like me, and I was dumbfounded. So many barbershop haircuts and biceps and work boots. There were ponytails too, and cornrows, and three-piece suits. Older butches who made me feel like I was still just a kid, and little baby butches that made me remember when my jeans fit like that. Every possible variation on butch, in all sizes, and many colours.

I remember thinking this is what straight, athletic men must feel like at a hockey game, but then realized that actually they get to feel like this all the time, so in fact it was not the same thing at all. Not the same thing as waiting forty years to be just one among the many.

An hour or so earlier, I had rolled my luggage into the marble foyer, convinced I had the wrong hotel. Everything was so spotless and fancy; I could not imagine four hundred butches descending upon this sterile place. The valets were all in red uniforms. The Muzak was soothing, if you were into panpipes. I was almost surprised when the well-groomed woman behind the counter found my reservation.

I got into the elevator with a dashing, salt-and-pepper-haired black man with an immaculately trimmed moustache and stylishly thin beard. The man smiled widely at me and nodded hello.

"You here for the conference too?" The handsome woman I had mistaken for a handsome man had a rich, deep, but unmistakably female voice. Not the honey-over-gravel timbre I have come to love from my trans male friends. Something different in the tone of her voice. Something familiar, too.

I nodded, and leaned up against the elevator wall. I was in the right place after all. Exactly the right place, in fact. I breathed in the smell of her cologne, let my eyes fall over her a little, trying not to look like I was noticing her pressed dress shirt and pants, her perfect silver and black beard and moustache, the shine on her shoes, her wide shoulders and short square nails.

"My name is Grey." She extended a long-fingered hand for me to shake. "So I'll see you tonight at the meet and greet then?"

I cannot capture in one thousand words or less exactly what transpired for me during the four days that followed, and what the experience meant for me. I could never describe the heart balm that I felt spending four days surrounded by everything and everyone butch, so I will just relate a few highlights.

Art all over the place, by butches, about butches. Photographs, paintings, films, the works. Not just a fleeting glimpse of a sort of butch. Not butch as the butt of a joke. Not a straight girl playing a butch on TV. Not a watered-down version of butch made palatable enough for mainstream taste buds. Real images and depictions of people who looked a whole lot like me. A glimpse at my own history. Proof that we have always been here, and evidence that we intend to continue to exist.

An all-butch tap dance ensemble. Need I say more about how great this was?

A multi-generational all-butch panel discussion. Hearing a seventy-three-year-old butch woman talk about seducing women during the war. And by the war I mean the Second World War. This was also one of the discussions I found most difficult to sit through. One of the panelists came of age in the seventies, and was what some would call a decidedly second-wave feminist lesbian separatist. She had what I found to be a lot of hateful things to say about my trans brothers, and patronizing and narrow-minded things to say about my femme sisters. I guess it was naïve to think we were just all going to get along. I squirmed in my seat, my blood starting to boil. My new friend Grey was right beside me, and she leaned towards me so we could whisper.

"I want her to shut up right now. She is being so divisive. We finally get a chance to come together and she is trying to pit us all against each other. Listen to her, she is spewing hate," I whispered between clenched teeth.

Grey tipped her head to one side, took a deep breath. Placed her palm on my leg, peaceful.

"You are mistaking fear for hate. Look at her. All I see is her fear. She is so afraid of disappearing." Grey spoke in that smooth, deep voice of hers, the one I had already learned to love.

Later I heard an old-school butch in a dapper suit give a keynote speech on feminism. She got a standing ovation before she even started talking, and another when she was finished.

And then there was all the talking. We talked in workshops, in the gym, in the halls outside our hotel rooms, over breakfast, lunch, dinner, and late-night drinks. We talked about chivalry and non-monogamy and history and politics and sex and sexuality and femmes and faggots and boxers versus briefs. What was most amazing for me was the stuff we didn't need to talk about. That was what touched me most, I think. Everything I didn't have to say, all the things that didn't need explaining. I didn't worry about being understood or believed, because for the first time in my life I was surrounded by other butches. And they just knew.

Throwing in the Towel

Sometimes you say things without really thinking. Sometimes you write things on Facebook without really thinking about the nine hundred people who will read them.

It all started with the towels. Not just any towels, mind you. These were brand new, fresh out of the laundry, white, pristine, and über-fluffy. I had just stepped out of my claw-foot bathtub in my new-to-me bathroom in my recently painted apartment and into the softest, most absorbent and slightly lemony scented towel this forty-year-old ass has ever felt. That towel wicked the moisture away from my butt like a dream. It felt better than my mother's towels. Better than a fancy hotel towel, even, mostly because it was mine and I knew for a fact mine was the first ass it had ever wicked water from.

It's the little things, right? I sat my luxurious towel-wrapped ass down at my desk in front of my computer and wrote, "My new towels are so fluffy and absorbent. I feel like a queen. A queen, I tell you." And then I hit "share."

Within minutes, the comments started to roll in. My lady friends all concurred. Some of my butch friends, well, not so much. One of them called me big old girl. One told me I needed some butch bonding time. A small debate ensued. A femme friend of mine suggested we all conceptualize fine linens as a high quality tool, used to entice fine ladies into your bathtub. We riffed some about stereotypes. I thought it was over.

The next day, I hung the freshly hemmed and pressed, sand-coloured velvet draperies in my living room, and stood back to appreciate how well they complemented the dark olive accent wall and the bone-white window trim. What can I say? It has pretty much been five years since I have had a stable, solo, sexy roof over my head. I am nesting. I sat at my desk and wrote: "Enjoying my new draperies like I do does not make me any less butch."

And again with the stream of comments. One of my friends responded that butches were supposed to keep thoughts like that to ourselves. Someone said that draperies could be butch as long as there were no pink bows on them. Someone else suggested that we needed a word for a butch metrosexual. This began a longer discussion on the various types of butch: soft butch, stone butch, old school, fag butch, gentlebutch, dandy.

I should say that all of this was fairly good-natured, and everyone's feathers went for the most part unruffled, at least on the page. But something about the whole discussion bugged me, and it got me to thinking about it all.

My first question was for myself. Why did I care if my butchness was called into question anyway? In my whole entire life I have never felt anything but butch, even before

I knew the word. That is certainly the way the world views me (going mostly on what rednecks call me from passing truck windows) and how my lovers place me on the fuck-ability spectrum. So why did someone I barely knew calling me a girl and suggesting I needed some butch bonding time chap my tender ass so much? Perhaps it was all those soft towels making me more thin-skinned than usual? And what was up with my butch brothers and sisters? I re-read the comments. Most of the femmes who responded maintained that the word butch didn't need adjectives or qualifiers: just butch would do the trick. It was mostly butches who were uncomfortable with my love of fluffy towels and draperies, and mostly butches who felt the need to further categorize ourselves.

One of the femmes who responded posed the following: "There's also an element of internalized homophobia in all of this. Maybe it's a conceptual leap but it seems to me that the notion that a 'real' butch can't like a fluffy towel or use words coded as feminine to describe her-/him-/hir-self isn't that far from the idea that it's not okay for boys to play with dolls. Are queer masculinities (or whatever you want to call them) so fragile? Their beauty, diversity, and resilience over the generations prove otherwise."

I thought about it all some more. Thought back to being eight years old, and frozen in the girl's dressing room at the ladies' wear store on Main Street in Whitehorse. My aunt was getting married and my mom was insisting that wearing anything but a dress to the wedding would be rude and she wasn't going to tolerate any more arguments from me about how dressy my brown corduroy suit could really be with the right blouse. I was being forced to try on this yellow and grey dress. My mom and the shop lady were looming outside the dressing room door, taking turns cajoling and threatening me to come out and show them how I looked. My guts were in my throat and all the moisture in my mouth was now collecting in my eyes. I was seriously too humiliated to open the door and come out. I was afraid of the wrath of my mother, and scared of the scorn of the saleswoman, but I was even more terrified of how vulnerable and wrong I felt in my body, in my skin, in my life in that dress. It wasn't just that I didn't want to be a girl. And it wasn't as easy as just wishing that I was a boy. It was the horrible realization that I was facing a world where there were no clothes for me because I didn't fit the world.

So I don't think that butch fear of our own femininity is all that simple to unravel. It is not just our own misogyny that makes us see anything less than manly as weak or less than. Our fear of our own inner girl is so much more complicated than that. Most of us grew up uncomfortable not only in our clothes, but in our pink bedrooms, our gender roles, our families' expectations, and even our own skins. We had to fight to find ourselves in all of that. And sometimes that makes it hard to drop all that armor and just sit back and enjoy the fucking draperies.

On Angels and Afterlife

On November 29, 2009, Catherine White Holman, my friend of seventeen years, was killed in a plane crash. It seems unreal to me still, even as I write these words. She was so beloved by so many, how could truth be so cruel, so unfair and brutal?

The two weeks following the tragedy were a blur of tears and grief and joy and old friends and buried hatchets and community. Catherine was known for her enormous heart, and the evidence that her heart is still beating in all of us is everywhere: the amazing army of friends and family who gathered immediately, the crowd of souls who sent so many condolences that it crashed the website, the several hundreds of mourners who lined the candlelit streets and filled the WISE Hall in Vancouver's East End for an eight-hour wake the likes of which even this Irish Catholic kid has never seen. All of this shone a light on how much she brought to this world, and just how much she will be missed. All of this is a sign of the passing of a truly remarkable woman.

This year was grief-heavy for me. My beloved gran,

Florence, passed away in May, and then Catherine, who truly was one of my very favourite ladies in the whole wide world. I have studied loss these last few months, and pondered the giant questions of life. I am told that Catherine did not believe in a life after death, though this is something I never discussed with her. I know for certain that my gran believed in heaven, and if there is anything resembling a great reward in the sky, then I know of no souls more deserving than these two women. The Catholic sisters at my gran's funeral confessed to me that they looked to Flo when their own faith wavered, as my gran's never, ever faltered. As a counsellor, Catherine leaves behind thousands of people whom she helped find a doctor or housing or treatment, or simply just listened to; people who swear that she saved their lives. If you ask me, if they both are not angels right now, then there is no such thing.

As for afterlife, I know what I would like to believe, and I know what I feel. There is no evidence of a heaven, but I do see traces of an afterlife every single day. I believe that people live on in the people who live. It's as simple as that. My gran lives on in me every time I recycle a Ziploc bag, every day that I work hard, every time that I reach out to care for my family, every time I remember to be grateful, every time I remember my scarf and gloves, every time I eat the leftovers instead of letting them go to waste. Every time I eat a raspberry hard candy and stuff a used Kleenex into my jacket pocket. Every time I light a candle, she is there in me.

Catherine helped me through some rough times. Several

years ago, I dragged a friend of mine off the streets and kept her home with me for a couple of weeks while she cleaned up and tried to get into a recovery program. Everyone else told me I was crazy, that my friend was a drug addict and a fuck-up and that I was just enabling her, keeping her from hitting bottom. Everyone told me the best thing I could do was nothing, and let my friend eventually help herself. So I went to see Catherine. She showed me into her little office in Three Bridges, and busted out a fresh box of Kleenex. I explained to her that I had been calling every morning for thirteen days trying to get my friend into detox, but by the time a bed finally became available I was informed that she was too clean for detox and now was on a sixty-day waiting list for a bed in a treatment house. I told her I could barely sleep because of the stress, and was afraid to leave my house in case the people my friend owed money to caught up with her; I was afraid of being robbed, or worse. She took out a binder and told me to call this place and talk to this guy, not that guy but this guy, to tell him Catherine said so. She told me who to call and where to go and what to do. And then she let me cry at her little coffee table for an hour. She told me I was a good friend, that I was doing the right thing, that everybody needed someone who wouldn't give up on them. She knew my friend too, and loved her at least a little, I think. She told me that if the roles were reversed, my friend would do the very same thing for me, and that no one would ever get clean without someone who believed that they could. And then where would we be?

So. This is what I know about an afterlife. Every time

you remember to smile with your whole damn face, Catherine lives in you. Every time you welcome a stranger to the party. Every time you laugh with your whole body, every time you love with your whole heart. Every time you dress up in your finest. Every time you flick back your long silver hair and get that twinkle in your eye. Every time you cry at a good story. Every time you drink tequila and smoke on your porch in your chair. Every time you wink at a cute butch. Every time you ride on the back of a motorcycle. Every time you stick up for the underdog, the unlucky, the disenfranchised, the addicted, the people whose family forgot them, the undervalued and the misunderstood, Catherine lives in you. Every time you keep the peace, keep the faith, keep on keeping on. Every time you sing in the truck. Every time you fuck who you want where and how you want to without fear or shame or reservation, Catherine White Holman will be smiling at you from somewhere. This I know for sure.

Somebody told me at the memorial that the only way we could make up for losing a heart the size of Catherine's is to put all of ours together.

My friend and neighbour saw me in the hallway of my building the other day, puffy-eyed and numb. He said something I would like to remember. Something I will repeat. He said, "I never know what the right thing to say is in these times, but I'm almost always around, and I got two ears to listen."

I reckon that's a pretty good start.

Uncle Ivan's Broken Hearts' Club Plan

Years ago I decided to do myself a favour and quit trying to figure out what she sees in him. You know her, too. You probably know several hers. The beautiful, talented, productive woman with all of her shit together, except for the lump on the couch she calls a boyfriend. She somehow manages to get both kids dressed and fed and off to school with their lunches packed, just in time to wake him up for the third time before she leaves for work, so he doesn't sleep in and miss his job interview that her friend lined up for him. You know and love some version of her. You've met and tolerated at least one or two variations on him.

For some reason, over the last two months or so, I know of at least three cases where he, for some unfathomable reason, dumped her, and here is the real mystery for me, she is left broken-hearted. Devastated even. I am not even going to get into a feminist analysis of why she still believes that she deserves no better than him, or that she feels undesirable unless he says otherwise, or why she has been socialized to take care of things that he should be man enough to do himself, because that has all been done. What I am going to do is write down the steps to heart recovery that she (and she, and her) and I came up with on the road to repair.

Step One. Get up. Do it now. There you go. I know he is a prick who called you from the airport to tell you he wasn't coming because he decided to take the Greyhound south with the singer who hired him to do the guitar tracks on her new record and now you have a matching tattoo with no match, but get up. You have important things to do.

Step Two. Go out and buy yourself the nicest matching bra and panties set you can afford. Yes, they must be matching. Yes, they must be sexy. You are going to see them, that's who. And if that isn't good enough, please refer to step five.

Step Three. You need new sheets. Yes, you do. Brand new sheets that have no memories in them. Again, get the best that you can reasonably afford. My friend Mary highly recommends the bamboo sheets; though pricey, she maintains that "they give you the silkiness of satin without all that slip sliding of pillows, and the bunching and wrinkling." Lucky for you, the sales bins at the Bay arc full of sheets on sale after the holidays. I just saw a real cute set of flannel sheets with a vintage flower pattern for twenty bucks. Why? Because if you are going to lay in bed soaking your pillow with tears (also a part of this process, though not listed here as a step) then it should be in no less than 450 threads per inch.

Step Four. Get some exercise. Ever wondered why the words exercise and exorcise are only a vowel away? Think about it. Not only will this make you physically feel better and help stave off depression, but in six to eight weeks when you accidentally run into him while he is coming out of the liquor store and you are returning with fresh kale from the organic foods market, you will be glad you did. Because when you turn on your patent heel and walk away, he is going to be sorry for himself because he is no longer tapping that beautiful ass. I know he broke up with you so he could pursue his spiritual path, which turned out to be code for fucking his twenty-three-year-old yoga student, but believe me you, six weeks is more than enough time for him to figure out that it doesn't matter that she can put both legs behind her ears when she still keeps her stuffed animal collection on her futon and she is leaving him for a girl in her second-year women's studies class anyway. But guess what? It is too late. You look fabulous, and you are going to take that beautiful ass and sashay away with it, all the way back to your apartment, where you finally got the smell of skunkweed out of the drapes.

Step Five. Get some beautiful new cock up in you. Preferably one attached to someone who is leaving town tomorrow. Do not date this cock. Do not give this cock your cell number. Do not get to know this cock's hopes and dreams. Ideally, this cock and you do not even speak the same language. In a perfect world, whoever owns this cock has to be on a plane within twenty-four hours, to a place you have no interest in visiting. Good. Now only remember this cock when you are practicing to become a professional masturbator. In your brand new sheets, of course.

Step Six. Do that one home renovation that you have been meaning to get around to for years. Paint that bathroom, or clean out that closet. Transform at least one thing in your living space. Do it alone.

Step Seven. Go to the hairdresser. Then, manicure, pedicure, facial. I have never done this last bit myself, but I have it on good authority that this is a crucial step. This can be done alone, or with up to twelve girlfriends. Libations to follow.

Step Eight. Take up a new hobby. Yes, in addition to masturbation. This is a great time to take that quilting class, or motorcycle maintenance course. Buy art supplies. Use them. Learn how to play again.

Step Nine. Call up all your old friends. Especially the ones who you quit hanging out with because he didn't like them. See them. Let them remind you how awesome you really are. Laugh about some stupid shit you did in high school until you snort bubble tea out of your nose by accident and you almost pee a little.

Step Ten. Be sexy. Whenever and wherever you want. For you, this time.

The Butch Version

Recently I wrote a piece for my (mostly) straight lady friends, listing the top ten steps to getting over your ex. This was an entirely communal endeavor: earlier that week I had solicited ideas through an open call on my Facebook page, so much of the advice came from recently single women themselves. This is a relatively new method of research for me, and a fascinating one, because like many folks who work in the public eye, quite a few of my Facebook friends are people I have never actually met in real life. Some I have now developed online friendships of a sort with, others not so much. This made me wonder: when it comes to human heart related stuff like community, or support, or advice, or friendship, is the quality of the connections forged between people any less real life if it happens online? Is the advice given by one stranger to another online any less helpful than it would be if delivered by a neighbour, or an old friend? Is face-to-face consolation somehow more tangible and meaningful than it is on Facebook, or from a phone call? All this got me to thinking. I haven't come up with any brilliant insights really, but still, there was a bit of thinking happening.

After my advice to recently single ladies came out, I received quite a few requests for a butch version of the ten steps to getting over the ex, so I put out another call on Facebook. I am going to pass on the most often repeated tips, and the steps that general consensus revealed to be helpful. But given the nature of some of the comments I received, I guess I need to include a bit of a disclaimer. When I say going to the gym and or getting some exercise will make you feel better, both physically and mentally, I am not insisting that everyone conform to mainstream advertising's ideal body type, nor am I eschewing any kind of height-weight-specific standards of what is sexy. I mean that going to the gym or getting some exercise will make you feel better. And when I say going out for libations with your pals can help you renew old friendships that might have gone to fallow while you were in an unhappy relationship, I am in no way making light of the seriousness of substance abuse, nor am I maligning anyone in recovery. I simply mean that going out for a beverage of your choice with other consenting adults whose company you might enjoy could be a pleasurable alternative to staying home by yourself and staring at the dents in the rug where the furniture used to be. So here are some of the tips to getting over a breakup, butch style.

Get a haircut. A fresh three pack of white T-shirts and new boxers were also popular suggestions. Other butch accoutrements can help, too: vintage cufflinks, a pocketknife, or a fountain pen can put a little bounce in your step and a sparkle in your eye.

Road trip. This one is a must. There was some debate over solo versus with the buddies. I think this is a personal choice. Whether it is a train ride through the prairies alone or five fellows piling into the van for a three-day, mostly naked camping trip, everyone agreed that a change of scenery is in order.

Messy food. Barbecue, crab, lobster, corn on the cob, fondue, fried things in general. Food that gets on you while you are getting it in you. Food that involves fingerbowls, rolls of paper towels, bibs, or even a hot shower afterward.

Going places with your dog in your truck. The hardware store to buy building supplies is a great idea. This is also the precursor to one of the most important steps of all: building something awesome. Shelves. A woodshed. A loft bed. A combination couch and bench press station. Doesn't matter what it is, it just matters that you build it. Nails should be pounded. Things should be sawed. Small amounts of blood need to be shed. This is a rite of passage, a vital ritual. Building something is also an excuse for another important step, which is:

Buy something pretty. Such as anything made by Bosch or Snap-on. This is where the discussion got a little heated: Milwaukee and Dewalt fans had to get a word in. Again, I believe decisions like this are a personal choice, and I for one would never get in between a brother and his or her tool preference. Some things are just too sacred.

Music. The stuff you want, and loud. Set up the subwoofer you found in the alley or at that garage sale and crank it. For me, this step is all about the classic rock, but that is just me. The same guidelines stated above for tool preference also apply here. What is important is that you create a new soundtrack for your life, starring you. Singing in the truck is also necessary. When the teenagers at the stoplight point and laugh, roll the window down and explain that your stereo is in fact yours, not borrowed from your mother, so you are inherently cooler, even if you are rocking out to Fleetwood Mac.

Manage what you say about your ex. This will affect the way things go for you. Be a gentleman, no matter how hard she makes it for you. This will pay off in the long run.

The most important step, in my opinion, is also the hardest. Build the brotherhood of butches. Reach out to your butch and trans male friends, and consciously seek out new ones. This is not a tired and sexist "bros before hos" thing, not at all. I am talking about building a strong, healthy community who can be there for each other. We have been taught to see each other as competition for too long, and we have suffered for it. We need to learn to stick together better. Because single is not such a bad thing to be, when you are not so alone.

She Shoots, She Scores

I'll admit it, I had a tear in my eye when the Canadian women's Olympic hockey team won the gold medal in Vancouver. I am not ashamed to tell anyone I spent a good portion of the Canada-US Women's game on my knees in the living room in front of my television, that I spilled my Diet Coke on myself when we were killing a penalty, and that I didn't miss a single game the whole series. I am a hockey fan, like so many Canadians are. We take our hockey pretty seriously. But I also take women's hockey personally.

I started playing hockey in the boy's leagues in the Yukon when I was six. I had played a couple of months of ringette, which is kind of like hockey but "for girls." You play with a rubber ring and a sawed off hockey stick without a blade and usually in your figure skates. Ringette is kind of ... well, not quite hockey. The coach of my ringette team happened to be shacked up with the coach of a boy's team, and when he happened to see me play he realized I was better than a couple of the boys on his team, and my career in the boy's league was born. I was the only girl (for lack of a more appropriate word) in the entire Whitehorse Minor Hockey League until I was sixteen. I was a decent

114

player, not a star, but quick on my feet and a good passer. Foreshadowing for a future life of passing? Perhaps.

The locker room situation was always an issue, especially on game nights, when one change room was occupied by my team, and the other by the opposition. Game nights I changed alone in the janitor's room, lacing up my skates by myself in the tiny, too quiet closet, usually next to a stinky mop bucket, in between a stack of puck-smeared pylons and a pallet of cardboard boxes full of plastic beer cups for the concession stand. When all the boys on my team were suited up, someone would come and knock on my door and I was then permitted to join my team in the locker room for our pre-game pep talk. I always felt like I wasn't quite invited in, like my presence was just being tolerated. One of my coaches nicknamed me "Token." I did not play hockey on a boy's team because I wanted to be a boy. I played hockey on a boy's team because I loved to play hockey. There were no other options available. When I turned sixteen, I was forced to quit playing with the young men. The guys my age were now substantially bigger ad heavier than me, and due to the threat of serious injuries from body checking and liability issues, the minor hockey league decreed that I go play on Whitehorse's fledgling and only women's team. This would have been in the mid-eighties, and although there were several excellent women players, there were also some who were just learning to skate. There was only the one team in town, and we had to travel to Alaska for an actual game. Coming from the competition and speed of the boy's games I had left behind, women's hockey was no comparison. I played ice hockey for a total of eleven years, and never once did I truly get a chance to really play with my own peers.

Now when I watch the Canadian women play, it somehow soothes an old slapshot sting left on my soul. I watch a full team of world champion calibre women playing my beloved game in front of a capacity crowd of screaming fans, and truly it makes my heart pound with new possibility. What I am witnessing now simply did not exist at all when I was a young player. I hear a little girl in the huge Olympic crowd being interviewed on the CBC. What does she want to be when she grows up? A women's hockey player, she answers, without a heartbeat of hesitation. This is no longer a crazy dream of a lonely kid in a northern town. This is now a good answer.

My Grandma Pat turned ninety on the day we won that gold medal. I called her that night. She had been glued to the television for the entire Olympics, she told me, which I found surprising. She confessed that she had been a speed skater when she was a little girl, which I had not known, and that even now she still remembers how much she liked the feel of having strong leg muscles.

I told her I knew exactly how she felt, that one of the things I liked about sports was that it was one arena where women were rewarded for speed, strength, and even muscle.

She turned down the volume on the television so we could really talk. "When I watched those girls win that hockey game today, I sat here and felt a remarkable thing. I have always thought life would have been better if I had been born a male. I could have made more money, done more things. I could have had more sexual freedom, or at least not have been judged so harshly for the sexual freedoms I took. I turned ninety years old today, and for the first time in my life I felt proud to be a woman. I watched them take their helmets off and they were ladies underneath, and I felt so proud of us."

I agreed with her. I didn't tell her that I suspected the US team in particular had been directed to wear makeup (my femme friends tell me the eyeliner jobs were obviously amateur work, performed by beginners) and grow their hair to straighten up a little. I didn't comment on how the American coach could barely bring himself to shake hands with the unflinchingly butch coach of the Canadian team. I did not bring up the fact that one of the American players had made the international lesbian sign with both hands directly into the camera shortly before begrudgingly bending her neck to accept her silver medal. I agreed with my grandmother, and reveled in my own remarkable sensation. Saying the words women, hockey, and myself in the same sentence, and for the first time in my life feeling included. Like I could belong there.

Only Two Reasons

Ever heard of a place called Pink Mountain? Population 100, maybe, and that is in the summer. About 180 clicks north of Fort St. John. One of those places on the road north that sells gas and propane and bad coffee and T-shirts for tourists. It was the morning of day three of the drive home from Vancouver to Whitehorse, and I pulled over in Pink Mountain for breakfast. Nothing much doing there, even by northern standards. You can get a tire fixed and buy an Alaska Highway hunting knife with a fake bone handle made right there in China and enjoy a burger with gravy from a powder and mushrooms from a can and cheese from a wrapper and fries from a freezer bag. The kind of place where they turn old bald truck tires into a flower planter and nail up licence plates for wall decorations.

I used the pay phone to check my cell phone messages because I hadn't had a signal since two hours outside of Prince George, and then slipped into a squishy booth and ordered breakfast. My neck was sore from sleeping sideways in the cab of my truck and when I rubbed it I discovered a crunchy spot of dried blood behind my ear from a black fly bite. Two truckers leaned back from their dirty plates, thumbs hitched behind belt buckles, toothpicks bouncing as they bullshitted back and forth across the table, a halo of cigarette smoke swimming in the sunlight above their heads. Sound of air brakes on the highway, and somewhere a dog barked, and another answered him from farther off in the scruffy pine trees. Smell of bacon cooking and wood smoke.

The waitress slammed into the dining room through the swing doors with three plates balanced on one arm and a coffeepot in her coffeepot hand. She deposited two of the plates in front of the tourist couple in the corner, and the third she slid on to my table while she simultaneously topped up my coffee and dropped three more creamers into the bowl next to the sugar jar.

"Can I get you anything else, honey?"

"Just the road report." I squinted up at her.

"North or south, darlin'?"

"North."

"Ten clicks or so of new pavement going in this side of Watson Lake, fifteen-minute wait for the pilot car, maximum, and other than that it's pretty smooth sailing, from what they tell me, anyway. All the way to Whitehorse, far's I know. Where you headed?"

"Whitehorse. To see the family. Born and raised. Third generation," I told her. I always feel like I have to say this. To let everyone north of Williams Lake know I am not a third-year forestry student from Alberta or a Montreal hippie wannabe or an American bear hunter or the eldest child

119

of a German land baron. I always have to tell people I am a Yukoner. This still matters to me.

She didn't care. "Never been to Whitehorse. I'm from Sault Ste Marie." She rests the coffeepot on one hip, staring at the wall above my table like it was a mirror. I notice then that she has a French manicure.

"You ever get homesick?"

She snorts, shakes her head a little. "Have to have a home first to be sick for, don't you? I've been here seventeen years now. Never look back. I go to Edmonton with the girl-friends when I want a taste of the big city."

"How did you ever end up way up here, then, in Pink Mountain?" I took a sip of my coffee. It tasted like boiled chemicals with cream and sugar added.

"Honey, there are only ever two reasons anyone comes north, you should know that. Thought you said you were born here." She winked at me. She had a tiny white sliver of a scar on her upper lip, you could barely see it, unless her lipstick was worn down a little like it was right now, and you were really looking. "Only two reasons."

I raised my eyebrow in a question mark.

"Love, or money."

"Which one did you come up for?"

The waitress let out a quick bark of a laugh, and re-vealed the maze of lines around her eyes.

"Well, darlin', it started off as love."

Maiden Heart

I put this story together over the last ten or twelve years, and it is still full of holes. It is a true story in the same way that an old vase that is broken into pieces in the sink and glued back together holds water. Maybe, maybe not. But it is no less beautiful to look at. This is what I think I know.

On October 31, 1997, my father turned fifty years old. He and my mother had split up about two years earlier, and as far as any of us could tell, he was attempting to drink himself into an early grave.

As always, he never let all that booze get in the way of a solid day's work, so he was half in the bag and all the way inside a tanker he was welding on when the phone rang in the little office at the back of his shop. He hung his torch up on the ladder and climbed out to get the phone. It had been ringing all day. Big family and a big birthday. Big pain in the ass.

"Happy Birthday, Don." The woman's voice was husky, with a bit of a smoker's rattle.

"Um, thanks." He didn't know who she was, but he felt as though he should. Something in her voice told him he should recognize her. Not the sound of her voice, more like the way she weighted down her words, like they meant something.

They chatted a short while; how was he doing, did he feel old, that kind of thing. She cleared her throat, paused for a second.

"You don't even know who this is, do you?"

"Keep talking," he insisted, sitting up a little in his greasy rolling chair. "I'll figure it out any minute."

"I should hang up on you right now."

"No no no, don't. Don't hang up. I will never sleep again from wondering. Just give me a hint."

"You forgot our promise."

My father took a sharp breath, dropped the pencil he had been fiddling with onto his desk.

"Patsy?"

She didn't speak, but wasn't silent on the other end of the phone line; a small, animal-like noise escaped her throat by accident, and thirty years hung in the space between them for a long second.

He repeated her name, more sure this time. "Patsy Joseph?"

She nodded, but he couldn't hear her nod, so she swallowed and spoke. "Uh-huh. It's me. And you forgot our promise."

My dad tells me this story in his boat, in 2003. It is August. We are in the middle of Marsh Lake, trolling one of his sweet spots for lake trout.

Patsy Joseph was his very first real girlfriend, he tells me, and she was two years older than him. They had promised each other when she was seventeen and he was fifteen that they would call each other on their fiftieth birthdays, no matter where they were. He had forgotten hers, almost two years earlier. She hadn't. Hadn't forgotten him at all.

They started talking on the phone quite a bit, and soon it was every day. She had left Whitehorse when her father moved to Hope, outside of Vancouver. The two childhood sweethearts never wrote or talked on the phone, he was mostly working in the bush back then, and they lost track of each other. When Patsy came back in the summer of 1969 to look for him, she heard from one of her girlfriends that he had gotten one of the Daws girls pregnant, and that he was married, was building a house up in Porter Creek somewhere. Catholic girl, what else could he do but the right thing?

Patsy was devastated, and left town with a truck driver who told her she had pretty eyes. Ended up in Dawson Creek. Good a place as any. Got a job in an auto parts place, on account of how my dad always made her help him fix up his '53 Mercury Comet convertible and so she knew a little about cars. More than most women did back then anyway. So, she still worked at the auto parts place, yeah, thirty years later, and she still lived with the truck driver, only he didn't drive truck anymore, he was on disability because of his back and maybe he couldn't drive the long hauls like he used to, but he could still beat on her so they weren't really together, these last few years, she lived in the upstairs suite of their house and he lived on the ground floor, and she wanted to sell that house and be rid of him for good, but they couldn't, not with this market, and so there she was. She told my dad she still loved him, always had, that she still had his old letters and birthday cards and some photographs. Kept them hidden from the truck driver all these years. Jealous and mean, you know the type.

My dad and I share a weakness for a lady who needs help. It feeds something big and empty in us to arrive on the scene with a truck or jumper cables or a generator or wide open kind of dumb heart; we like to think it sort of makes up for always saying the wrong thing just when the song ends and the room goes quiet. My dad told his childhood sweetheart that he had not seen in over thirty years not to say a word to her ex-trucker, just to pack up her car when the guy was asleep, take only the stuff she really needed, and drive to work like it was any other day, and he would meet her there. He would take care of the rest. He would take care of everything. He would take care of her. And did she have snow tires?

The next bit of this story I heard much later, not in my dad's boat, but in his 1981 Ford F-150 pickup truck, driving in a full-on blizzard on our way back from spending the night in the little house in Atlin that he was building for when he and Pat finally retired. They had been married for about ten years. The windshield wipers thump-thumped in the quiet but merciless storm; snow devils swirled on the black ice in front of the two stab marks our headlights made into all that oblivion. Nobody but us crazy enough to be out on that road in this weather. Used to be when I was a kid I was never scared when my dad was driving, no matter how big the waves or black the ice. Now I am older. I light his smokes for him so he doesn't have to take his hands off the wheel for long. No streetlights here, just dark and snow and cold all around us, not even a light on in a cabin, not out here, not until we hit the main highway. His face is lit up only a little from the dashboard lights, and the cherry on his cigarette dangles in the dark when he talks.

He tells me how he drove almost all the way through the night, when he went south to go get her, and walked into the auto parts place in Dawson Creek in the early afternoon. She was behind the counter wearing an angora sweater, kind of light blue he thinks it was, and he tried not to let his face show it, but he couldn't believe how old she looked. She said it was time for her coffee break; did he want to come up to the lunchroom with her then? She wouldn't meet his eyes with hers, wouldn't look at him right on at all, kept hiding her face behind her bangs, which were still blonde, but shot all through with silver now. She told him much later she couldn't rest her eyes right on his face at all that day, not even for a second, because she couldn't believe how old he looked. Couldn't look right at the years in his eyes and stamped all over his face. So she stared out the window into the parking lot of the auto parts place even though there was nothing much to look at out there and she had seen it all a million times anyways, but it was better than turning around and seeing your beautiful memory grown old and wrinkled and grey and with a bit of a gut now. And my dad, he has never been any good at knowing the right thing to say, so he tells a joke. And she smiles at the joke, because he's funny, he really is, the old man is, and she turns to look at him just a little and then she laughs.

Light me another smoke, he tells me, and so I do, trying not to get any smoke in me at all because I quit for over a year now, which makes him not trust me in a way that neither of us can put our finger on.

"Anyway," he says, "that's when I saw her. The girl I fell in love with when I was a kid. She laughed, and all those years just fell away somehow, and suddenly it was just her and I standing there, together. So she quit her job and followed me home back to Whitehorse in her Lincoln Continental and I married her up at Nolan's reindeer farm with only an eight-fingered farm hand as a witness. Filthy old Danny Nolan is a justice of the peace, can you believe that? Didn't invite any of the family. Not even my brothers. John still hasn't forgiven me."

My father's eyes are shining with tears he will not allow to slip out and down his cheeks. He opens his window a crack and the wind sucks his cigarette butt out of his square-nailed fingertips and disappears with it. It was true. I had seen it for myself, the previous summer. I had seen Pat's face crack when she laughed and reassemble for a split second into a much younger memory of itself. Almost pretty. I can't even remember what the joke was, but I remember that face, remember wondering where it had come from, and where she hid it the rest of the time.

We finally make it to Whitehorse; the last fifty clicks into town we just trailed behind the snowplow, the storm swirling behind us and filling in our tracks as soon as we were gone. Pat has the coffee on, and all six of their dogs explode in a fit of barking when we stomp through the front door and strip off our wet parkas and heavy boots. Pat is pissed off, she is not saying anything but you can see it in her face. We shouldn't have been driving in that weather, and we both know it, so we say nothing.

I sit down at the little kitchen table and pour a dollop of evaporated milk into my coffee, add a sugar cube from the Roger's box on the counter. My dad is stoking the fire. The television is on but turned down so you almost can't hear it. She won't let him smoke in the house anymore, and it smells like the cinnamon-scented candle burning on the coffee table. There are several pictures that hang on the wall next to the bathroom, above the washer and dryer, right next to her Elvis clock. Pictures of the dogs when they were puppies, stuff like that. There is one of her and my dad, one she kept secret from her ex-trucker somehow, all of those awful years. She has had it blown up and framed. Black and white, my dad and her, back in the mid-sixties, he with his hair slicked back and his smoke pack tucked into the rolled up sleeve of his white crew neck T-shirt, his jeans with wide cuffs and his lips curled in a smile around his cigarette. She has a kind of beehive hairdo, and his arm is around her waist. They are standing in front of an old wall tent, and the chrome on the grill of the Mercury Comet winks in the sunlight beside them, and the soft shape of the mountain next to the Fox Lake campground rolls in the far background. The photo looks like something out of an old ad from *Life* magazine or something. This photo hangs right next to another one, this one in colour, a shot of the two of them again, her with her new perm and him with his silver shock of hair sticking up all over. He is wearing sandals and a clean work shirt with the sleeves pulled up over the welding scars on his forearms, and they are standing next to the Lincoln Continental, which is parked beside the motor home he traded a guy for some welding a couple of summers ago. In the background is the same mountain; they have returned to the very same campground site, it looks like, right there on the gravel beach of Fox Lake. But there was a forest fire there a couple of years ago, and so the trees left standing on the familiar shape of the mountain are crooked little blackened matchsticks, the fireweed curling up between them and taking over. My dad has a gut and his wife is squinting into the sunlight, her glasses catching a glint so you can't really see her eyes behind them. But none of this matters, really, because it is forty years later, and they are both smiling.

All About Herman

My grandmother has kept a journal for most of her life. All ninety years of it. She loves to write, she tells me on the phone from the Yukon. I can picture her, all the way from Vancouver, it is January, so she has the propane fireplace on in the living room and she is sitting with her legs tucked up beside her on the couch like she does. She is wearing a dress with a floral pattern and the rug needs a good vacuum, which she would do if she could still see the dirt, but she can't. There is the smell of drip coffee and bread dough set aside under a clean tea towel to rise. Newspapers and magazines cover the coffee table, and she has a fresh cup of black tea with cream and sugar in it on the side table, next to a plate empty save for a scattering of toast crumbs. She has lived in this little house on Elm Street in Whitehorse since 1967. It is the only house belonging to anyone in my giant family that has been there all of my life. Everyone else has sold and moved up, to make room for more kids, and later, less room for fewer kids. Only this house remains, as unchanged as playground concrete in all of our memories. I can't imagine my grandmother anywhere else but in this house, and I refuse to think about anyone else ever living here when she is gone.

"Did you get my envelope?" she asks me, as always speaking far too loud into the receiver, as though she doesn't quite trust in the technology. "I sent you a copy of all of my latest scribblings."

She has been going back through her old journals, editing them and typing them up. Her vignettes, as she calls them. She has been sending me envelopes, sometimes containing carefully folded, ten-page-long stories handwritten in her sloping but still solid script, sometimes typewritten in all capital letters, with capital Xs crossing out mistakes, and corrections made in blue pen in the margins. Most are untitled, with just that day's date in the upper right hand corner. I read and re-read them; they are full of old stories, confessions, and advice. Lately her musings have grown somehow more poignant, more emotional, full of regrets.

"What I bitterly regret are the things I didn't say, and the questions I didn't ask," she writes. "I have dreams now, and I dream of the past. I am not old. I'm not an old lady. I am young, vibrant, full of life. I'm like that in all my dreams. So I enjoy my dreams."

Her last letter was four pages long, typewritten. She has titled this one, called it "All about Herman." I don't remember Herman, as a child I knew of him only through escaped bits of stories whispered here and there, nobody talked about Herman much. He died Christmas Day in 1970; I never knew why. I knew next to nothing of the story of Herman until just last year, when my grandmother writes:

"It all started with the morning of March the 9th, 2008. It was his birth day on March the 9th, 1930. He has been dead now for thirty-eight years, and on this morning, I am thinking about him. I remember him, and a week or so later, I can't get him out of my mind."

Herman had been an engineer for the Department of Public Works, and my grandmother was a secretary. She was married; her husband and three of my uncles had recently left the Yukon and travelled ahead of her to New Zealand, where she was to join them in a year, when they had found work and set up a place for them all to live. My dad didn't want to leave the Yukon; he was already working, driving a caterpillar in the bush on a road building crew. My grandmother was to stay behind and save all the money from her government job. At least that was the plan. But that is only sort of what happened.

It turned out Patricia liked being alone. This was unforeseen.

And then the big, rugged engineer began to court her. At first she turned him down. Finally, she agreed to go for a drink with him one night. They began an illicit affair. He took her on trips. He liked classical music. He was well-read. He was in love. And she was in trouble.

Time did what it does, and the day came for her to travel to New Zealand and be reunited with her husband and sons. Herman travelled with her to Vancouver, and put her on a steamship. When she arrived at the little cabin she was to share with two other women for the journey, it was full of flowers Herman had sent her. Her cabin mates thought she was crazy to leave a man like that behind.

"I haven't any words to describe my disappointment

when I arrived in Auckland. The boat docked, and there he was. This husband of twenty-odd years that I was committed to spend the rest of my life with. He was there. He takes me home to a rented house, full of furniture bought on the hire-purchase, which I am supposed to get a job right away and pay off. He doesn't say I'm so glad you're here, welcome, I hope I can make you happy. He doesn't say any of those things. He just spreads the newspaper out on the table to look for jobs. For me. I do get a job. I am hired as office manager, switchboard operator, and tea lady. One of the mistakes I made was I used day-old milk; I also bought lemons when there was a lemon tree out in the yard, where I could have picked a lemon. Well, I had picked a lemon, twenty years ago.

"This was not a new life—just more of the same dismal, unhappy existence. Don, the man I had married, was not my friend. I began to dislike him, and that dislike eventually turned into hate. I had brought all of this onto myself. All right, I had allowed myself to have feelings for another man. How was I going to deal with that? Well, he dealt with it."

She eventually left Don and New Zealand, and returned to the Yukon alone. Her youngest son, John, would follow her in a year.

She tells me this part of the story forty years later, at her kitchen table, the part about how she pulled her car over to the side of the road in Cache Creek, at the crossroads, and pondered all those road signs for a long minute. Should she go back to the prairies, and her mother, or was it north she wanted? She claims she wasn't thinking of Herman so much in that moment. She tells me she thought it was over, that they had ended it. But she continued north, so I don't know if I believe her. I don't think it was me she was lying to. I'm no shrink, but I know enough to know when a woman most needs to believe her own lies first.

I get the story from her in snapshots, short bursts, late-night kitchen table talk when the lips are loose with the whiskey. I knew she returned to the north, it was why we were all still here. She tells me part of the story in 2004: she breathes out in one long sentence that my grandfather broke her nose in New Zealand. Just a detail, an aside in another story about something else. She doesn't rest on the memory, and I will myself not to react, so she won't lose her train of thought. She does that now, more and more. Yesterday on the phone she confesses that she never wrote to me much about what happened to her in New Zealand because she hates to remember it, wants her sons to hold a different past in their heads. A different father. My grandfather, and what he did.

"In a fit of pent-up bottled rage, he attacked me. I can't imagine his hatred, and anger that he would smash me in the face over and over again with his fist. The blood was spattered all over the wallpaper. He wanted to mess up my face, so that I wouldn't be attractive to another man. The kids were there, they knew what was going on. They saw it. They had to clean up the mess. Years later I asked Rob, I said what did you do about all that blood on the wall? He said, we cleaned it up."

Pat returned to Whitehorse, alone, and got herself a job. She stayed with friends of the family and made no attempt to contact Herman. But they ran into each other on Main Street.

"He must have thought he'd seen a ghost," she writes. "We didn't speak very much, but he didn't go away. He came back. He came to see me. This time this was serious. We resumed what we had started. I thought our relationship was private. I thought nobody knew. I thought it was a secret. I thought we were kinda sneaking. It was not private. Everybody knew. The whole town knew. I didn't have to make a secret of it anymore. I was acknowledged as his partner, and I started divorce proceedings.

"I realize now the seriousness of his drinking problem. Like he was two people. Dr Jekyll and Mr Hyde. The Dr Jekyll was a good natured, amiable, agreeable, softhearted, generous, loving ... what else can I say? But the Mr Hyde could be terrifying. He could charge at me like an enraged bull, and he was bigger, he was twice the size of me. He wasn't fat, he was just meaty. I probably should have been afraid of him, but I wasn't. Because I knew he wouldn't hurt me. The last thing in the world he would do would be to hurt me.

"He built that house, and I know he built it for me, I know he did. We tried to live in it, but it just didn't work. There was just too much. It was battle stations all the time. I know it was the drinking. He spent a lot of time in bars. The Capital Hotel. I was not allowed to go there, and I never went there with him.

134

"He talked of getting married, but this bothered me. I couldn't see that. But he told me that if I married him, he would give me a sapphire ring that would flash blue like my eyes did when I was mad at him. If that's a proposal, then I guess that's what it was.

"But it ended on Christmas Day, 1970. He collapsed in my house. Right there. Right there on the floor. A big, vital, alive man came crashing to the floor. I called the ambulance. In those days you didn't go with the ambulance, that wasn't done, you were in the way if you did. So I just hid in my second bedroom, I couldn't bear even seeing them taking him away. I didn't visit him until the next day. I went in there and I discovered that he had tried to walk out of the hospital. He had torn out his tubes and whatever they attach to you and tried to walk out. I thought this was probably a good sign that maybe he was going to be all right. Even when somebody said to me how's Herman doing? I said I think he's out of the woods. I said that. He was anything but out of the woods.

"That night I got the call about three o'clock in the morning that he had died. He was forty. Forty years old. The same age as you?

"But had he lived, he would be eighty-one today. He'd probably be as mean as sin. In a way, I am glad he never lived to see me grow old. I'm glad in a way. Because he wouldn't have been very nice about it. He would have been cruel. All in all, we were together about five years. I was as happy as I've ever been in my life.

"Which brings me back to March, 2008. I feel his

presence. I don't believe in spirits. I can't imagine him going to heaven. He just wouldn't fit in. And the thought of me having to spend eternity with him in heaven? I'd rather not. We would just fight.

"You should only marry for two reasons. Only two reasons. Love or money. I know what real love is now. And what I had for Herman, there was nothing like it before him, nor has there been since. Passion helps. I mean it helps. It's the glue that holds the love together. Well, all right, sex. Let's face it. My love affair with Herman was passionate. Even when we fought, it was passionate. I think it can actually outlive death, and even time. In retrospect, I believe this. Now, I am ninety. Like sweet ninety and never been kissed? I still feel the same way about him that I did forty years ago. Believe it or not, that is the truth. He told me he liked to hold my little hand. Somehow, I'd like to think he still does."

Just a Love Story

A couple of years ago I was crammed into a Honda Civic hatchback with four poets, squinting through the furious wiper blades to find the right exit off of the Number One Highway into Surrey. We were on our way to a suburban high school for a gig.

The slam poet in the back seat with the relentless bad breath squeezed his face into the front seat. "It's Valentine's Day tomorrow. I think we should all do love poems."

There was an exuberant round of agreement from everyone but me. I cracked the passenger window just a little, and an icy spray of February rain hit my cheek. I took a deep breath and rolled the window back up. I was the only storyteller in the car. I am used to this. Used to being lumped in with the poets. This doesn't bother me. I have even stopped telling people I have never written a poem in my entire life. Storyteller, poet, close enough, I guess, for most people. Even though they are not the same thing at all.

"I can't read a love story in a high school in Surrey," I blurt out, feeling a bit like a parent who just busted in on a pillow fight.

"Why not?" the slam poet heavy-breathed from the back seat, his eyebrow raised in a question mark.

I was also the only queer person in the car. I am used to this. This almost never bothers me. Gay person, straight person, what is the difference anymore, right? Aren't we over all that?

Truth is, I have been over it for decades now. Most of us mostly are. But not in a high school. And not here in Surrey, British Columbia. Surrey, where they banned the *Harry Potter* books from school libraries for encouraging witchcraft. They also banned *Heather Has Two Mommies* and *One Dad, Two Dads, Brown Dad, Blue Dads* for promoting anti-family values.

"Because," I say, letting out a long breath, "it is scary enough to be a homo in a high school in Surrey in the first place."

His face shows no sign of recognition, of understanding, of camaraderie, and I suddenly feel in-my-bones tired.

I take another heavy breath. "For you, a love poem is just that. A love poem. And I am glad for you, I truly am. But for me to read a love poem in a high school in the bible belt is a political statement, whether I mean it to be or not, someone will think I am recruiting, armpits will grow moist with tension, I will be pushing the homosexual agenda on unsuspecting adolescents, I will be disrespecting someone's interpretation of the words of their God, you know, the whole tired routine."

"So what?" pipes up the anarchist beat poet who had been slumped in the backseat beside the slam poet. "We've got your back, Coyote, fuck them all, rock the boat. Surrey needs it."

"What if I just want to tell a love story?" I asked. Only the thump of the windshield wipers responded.

I met her the first time eight years ago, in the hospitality room of the Granville Island Hotel, during the Vancouver International Writers' Festival. She was wearing tall red boots and her wool jacket and handbag matched. Silver and black ringlets surrounded her dimples and sparkling smart eyes. Some people you can see how brilliant they are from a distance, like there are little invisible sparks coming out of their brain while it is working, creating static electric charges in the air above their heads. She was electric spark smart, and all I remember is I could make her laugh. Every time she laughed, my heart pounded possibility. When I saw her from across the room, she kind of shone. Like God Himself was pointing her out to me with a glowing finger. I left with too many plastic glasses of free wine in my belly, and without her phone number in my pocket.

I ran into her on the Drive a couple of days later, just like I knew I would.

It was one of those early spring days in Vancouver, where all of a sudden the grey of the previous week gives way and suddenly it is raining cherry blossoms everywhere, a crushed and scented carpet of them underfoot. We were talking about music. Somehow the band Nirvana came up, I can't remember why, I like them all right, maybe they reminded me of some other band I liked better, I can't remember, but she told me that the album *Nevermind* was her favorite all-time record when she was in grade seven.

I quickly did some silent math in my head. How could the sexiest, smartest, silver-hairedest, woman I had ever met be too young for me to go out with?

"Grade seven?" I blurted out. "How can you be twenty-three? How did I get to be … if I had met you in 1991 when *Nevermind* first came out, you would have been …" I shuddered.

"Twelve years old." She laughed again. Like this didn't matter at all. "It's the grey hair, right? That fooled you? I started going grey when I was sixteen. Runs in the family."

My shoulders seemed too heavy to hold up all of a sudden. I told her I was too old for her. She told me that age doesn't matter. I told her the only people who think there is no such thing as too old for you are usually too young to know any better. She told me that she had just come out of the closet, that she wanted an older lover. She told me I was being ageist. I told her I used to think people were just being ageist too, when I was her age. She told me I was being ageist. I told her I know. Then I let out a long sigh. Did what I had to do. Told her that I was a dirty rotten rotter, that I had been around the block a million times, that I had slept with more women than … that I had slept with a fair number of women in my long and lucky life of loving, and that she should pick someone special, that this was her second chance at having a first time, and most people never get a second first-time chance at anything, that she was lucky, and not to waste that chance on a pussy crook like me. Go, I told her, and fall in love with a nice woman. Fall in crazy stupid dumb-struck love and move in together and figure yourself out, don't get a cat, though, and then fall out of love, suffer through a hopefully short but nevertheless nether-region-numbing bout of lesbian bed death, and break up. Lather, rinse, and repeat. I told her that if she still wanted me five years from now, to come and find me. I told her that if she still wanted me then, that I would be honoured. Told her I had to go, before I changed my mind.

I would see her around from time to time. Usually at poetry readings. Started going to a lot of poetry readings. Started dressing up to go to poetry readings. Started ironing my shirts to go to poetry readings.

Five years later I am in my car, waiting to turn left off of Commercial Drive onto First Avenue, on my way to the Home Depot. My girlfriend and I have recently broken up. We still live together, which could have been awkward, but luckily she was often in Portland with her new lover, who made more money than me, had a really hot truck, and a brand new Harley. So of course I was doing what any self-respecting butch does in this kind of situation: I was throwing myself heart-first into a complicated home improvement endeavour.

This next part seems like magic, but it is true. Some would say this is evidence that magic is for real. I was listening to classic rock and Fleetwood Mac was singing about don't stop thinking about tomorrow, and so I was thinking about tomorrow, about how maybe this breakup was for the best anyway, right, because look, I was finally going to get the new floor down in my office, and wasn't I now free to do what I wanted with whomever I wanted, plus, hadn't it been five years now, so couldn't I take that silver fox out on a date now? Thirty-eight and twenty-eight wasn't so bad, right?

And that's when I saw her. Standing on the corner with a coffee in her hand. Her hair now more silver than black, somehow even more beautiful. She waved when she saw me. I unlocked the passenger side door and she jumped in.

"Where you going?" she smiled, showing her one crooked tooth.

"Home Depot," I told her.

"I love Home Depot," she said, and winked.

We didn't get out of bed for three days. She did a lot of yoga, it turned out. I vowed to quit smoking, so I could keep up with her. Eventually, I did. Quit smoking, that is.

Last month we went home to the Yukon. My family loves her, especially my mother. I think she is actually the daughter my mother always wanted. She is so smart and dresses so fine and almost has her PhD and it almost makes up for my mom having me and my even blacker sheep sister as her real children.

I drove her out to one of my favorite places in the world, the Carcross Desert. White sand and mountains and so much sky all over the sky. Some dirt bikers had accidentally burned a huge heart shape into the sand with their back tires. We stood together in the centre of that accidental heart, and it seemed like the perfect spot to put that big old diamond ring on her finger.

My family is beside themselves. At dinner, my cousin Dan insists that I tell his sister the whole story of how we met. It's so romantic, he says. It is just such a love story.

IVAN E. COYOTE is a writer and performer. She is the author of five books published by Arsenal Pulp Press: the four story collections *Close to Spider Man*, (shortlisted for the Danuta Gleed Short Fiction Prize), *One Man's Trash*, and *Loose End* (shortlisted for the Ferro-Grumley Women's Fiction Award), and her latest, *The Slow Fix*, as well as the novel *Bow Grip* (also shortlisted for the Ferro-Grumley Women's Fiction Award and named a Stonewall Honor Book by the American Library Association). Ivan was a founding member of the performance collective Taste This, and is a long-time columnist for *Xtra!* in Toronto and *Xtra! West* in Vancouver. Originally from the Yukon, Ivan lives in Vancouver.